Perilous Pursuits

THE ARCHMAN (BOOK TWO)

This is a work of fiction. Names, characters, organisations, places, events, and incidents are either products of the author's imagination or are used fictitiously. Otherwise, any resemblance to actual persons, living or dead, is purely coincidental.

Self-published.

ISBN: 978-1-0692093-2-0 (print)
ISBN: 978-1-0692093-3-7 (digital)

Cover design byLeona-Brook (@leonabrookartist)

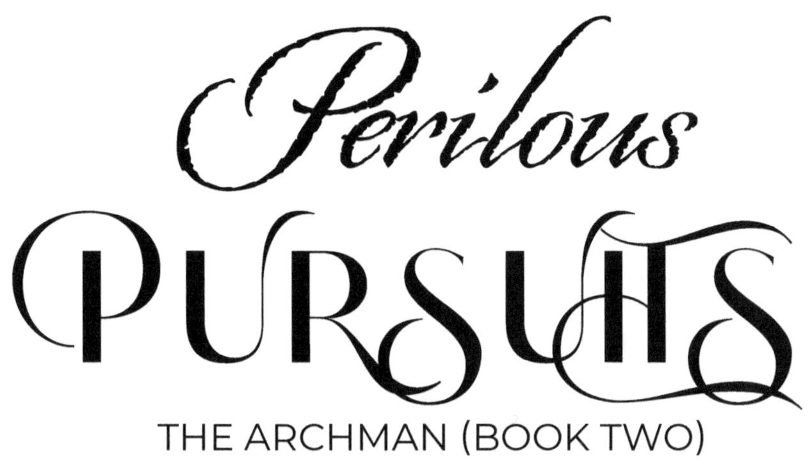

THE ARCHMAN (BOOK TWO)

THOMAS J.A. WATSON

Acknowledgements

This novel only exists thanks to the combined efforts of many people.

Thanks to the men of Cornerstone for holding me accountable to my goals and helping me to pursue my purpose.

Thanks to freelance copyeditor Stephanie Wilson for guiding me through the dark, uncharted territory of the editing process.

A special thanks to John, Jane, Hugh, and Blythe for your endless encouragement, and for the unique inspiration which I get from our profound conversations.

And, of course, I would like to thank everyone that has devoted their time and readership to *The Archman*. I really appreciate the support, especially since this is the first story I've published.

-Thomas J.A. Watson

Check out my website at thomasjawatson.com

You can find my other available works, segments for upcoming projects, and a blog which I update once a month.

CHAPTER

A GRAVE PROCEDURE

The Archman snaps around to the sound of Kinsley's pistol discharging. He is immediately overcome with a dismayed astonishment, his red eyes widening with a stunned stillness. Everyone freezes in their place as time grinds to a crawl, each second stretching on for a small eternity.

Kinsley's frothing spite has completely evaporated, replaced with a distraught shock. His arm is still holding out his smouldering flintlock pistol, his index finger still pulled back against the trigger.

Eira looks down and brings a hand to her abdomen, which is quickly being dyed in shades of deep red from a haemorrhaging wound in her stomach. She stands perfectly still, not completely registering what has happened. There is a split second of serenity before her body plunges her into a state of agonising torment, causing her to keel over instantly.

The Archman moves with an almost imperceptible swiftness, rushing to Eira and catching her before she collapses onto the deck. He looks down at her bloodied torso, alarmed and appalled by what he sees. He turns towards Kinsley, who is still frozen stiff with confusion.

The Archman's expression morphs from a shocked dismay to a conflagrating rage, aimed straight towards Kinsley. Frowning with a condensed malice, the Archman directs his vermillion glare right through Kinsley's defenceless psyche. He grits his teeth, exposing both his fangs with a predatory aura. His whole being inspires nothing but raw animosity.

The Archman's fearsome presence petrifies Kinsley to his very core. He drops his pistol and scrambles to his feet, exerting every ounce of energy he can to escape the Archman. Kinsley bolts across the deck, fleeing to the gangplank and back to the battleship.

The Archman watches him as he runs away. Part of him wants to give chase and hunt him down until he has Kinsley's neck between his fangs, but he has greater priorities right now. He looks back to Eira, who is bleeding out more and more by the second.

Eira clutches the right side of her abdomen, where the musket ball struck her. Her hands are already heavily stained with gore, which is dripping down onto the deck beneath her. Her breathing is sharp and shallow, rendered quick and uneven by the deluge of adrenaline pouring into her system. Her muscles contract and spasm uncontrollably as she falls deeper and deeper into a panicked anguish. She did not know her body was capable of such physical excruciation.

The Archman takes a full breath in, keeping his head as level as he can, given the circumstances. He lifts Eira up off the deck and runs as quickly and safely as he can below decks. As he lifts the hatch to go inside, he sees Kinsley's ship pulling away from them.

"Full masts now! Get that damn anchor up!" Kinsley bellows to the crew, still frantic and feverish from the Archman's glare.

The Archman throws the hatch aside and descends the two staircases hastily, cradling Eira in his arms carefully. She is shivering with a profound somatic misery.

A trail of blood drips onto the steps behind them as the Archman carries Eira through the artificially lit corridors. He arrives at a doorway, kicks it open forcefully, and walks inside.

Eira looks around, her already agitated state made worse by the fact she is now in the Archman's slaughterhouse.

The Archman sets her down gently on the steel table so she is lying on her back. Eira can see the hook on the ceiling dangling about three feet away from her. It is a distressing sight, though she finds solace in the fact she cannot imagine experiencing anything worse than what she is going through.

The Archman steps away from Eira and pulls back his hood as he rushes over to the wooden counter against two of the walls. He opens drawers and cabinets in a mad frenzy, pulling out implements and utensils which Eira is not able to make out from her narrowed peripheral vision.

Eira is not sure if the pain is getting worse, or if the hard metal table just does not provide the same relief as the Archman's muscular arms. Either way, everything is only getting more and more unbearable. All her nerves feel like they are on fire, spreading harrowing impulses across her whole body.

The Archman returns to her side, carrying several metallic implements that he sets down on the table next to her. Among them is a small glass bottle which he picks up and shakes a few times, jostling the opaque liquid contained within. Holding a thin metal tube with a glass chamber attached to the back, he plunges a metal needle into the cork of the bottle and pulls on two metal rings to draw the bottle's liquid into the glass chamber.

Eira watches the Archman working with the piece of fine gadgetry, confused and wary of his actions. She is sweating all over, the perspiration mixing with the blood from her stomach in a gruesome concoction of bodily fluids. She goes to take a breath but coughs several times before she can fill her lungs. Once she manages to take a proper breath, she looks up at the Archman as she works with tremendous effort to speak.

"A-am...am I—"

"Don't speak," the Archman dictates with a soft assertiveness. He looks down at Eira and places a hand on her shoulder.

"You're going to be alright. I promise."

For a brief moment, there is a respite from the pain in the wake of the Archman's words.

He takes the glass and steel apparatus in his right hand and brings it to Eira's right arm, which is closest to him. He rolls up the sleeve to her elbow, searching her forearm for a vein. He locates one which is quite pronounced and places the tip of the needle on it. With a smooth pressure, he slides the thin piece of metal through the skin, plunging it superficially into her arm. He pushes on a plunger in the back of the device with his thumb, injecting the liquid inside the glass chamber into her bloodstream.

Almost instantly, Eira feels a wave of relief wash over her, crashing down over her body and drenching her in chemical alleviation. The crippling pain from her abdomen has been reduced to little more than an irritable ache as every muscle, ligament, and tendon in her body relaxes at once. Just moments ago she had felt like she was teetering on the edge of mortality, but now she cannot be further from it.

The Archman pulls the needle out of her arm and sets it aside. Though her panic has completely melted away, the Archman is still working with an almost neurotic focus as he sorts through his instruments.

Once he has determined how he will proceed, the Archman grabs Eira's shirt in his hands and tears the front open with a vigorous tug. He tears away more of the fabric to uncover her chest and midriff, both of which are painted with sanguine shades of red.

Eira is a bit embarrassed having her breasts exposed in such a fashion, but with her life on the line, she finds it difficult to care about things like modesty or privacy.

The Archman brushes his silver hair out of his eyes so he can see better. He turns away and grabs a white rag from the countertop and starts blotting the blood from Eira's belly, cleaning up the wound slightly. The open lesion on her upper-right abdomen can become only so spotless, as blood still leaks everywhere.

He takes one of his metal implements from the table: a metal rod with a magnifying lens on it. He places it on the outside of her wound so the lens is hovering an inch above the opening. He takes a second metal rod and holds the gory puncture point open, analysing the totality of the damage. After a little while, he sets the instruments aside and gets to work.

Eira lifts her head slightly so she can watch the Archman while he works. He takes a thin sewing needle in one hand and a pair of pliers in the other. He inserts the hand tool into the weeping wound. It is quite a surreal experience for Eira, feeling the cold metal implement poking through her insides without any accompanying pain. It is the closest she has ever gotten to an out-of-body experience.

The pliers latch onto a hard surface in Eira's guts. The Archman pulls the pliers out, gripping the musket ball that was lodged in her abdomen. He drops the bloody piece of used ammunition on the table and returns the pliers to the inside of the wound. He takes the sewing needle and inserts it into the wound with surgical precision.

Eira watches in fascination as he runs the needle through some unknown part of her inner anatomy with perfect dexterity. Just as when he wields his sword, he employs an almost inhuman delicateness and exactness. His eyes remain glued to her body with an unflinching focus, his fingers working with a level of finesse that surpasses expertise. Though her body is almost entirely numb, she can just barely feel the calluses on his hands, which are covered up to his wrists in her blood.

Eira lowers her head back to the steel table, her fascination not able to keep up completely with her nausea. Unsurprisingly, she does not have much of a stomach for watching surgery being performed on herself, and it is especially hard considering that stomach had just been shot.

She closes her eyes and exhales. Despite her aversion to witnessing her own procedure, she still feels at ease. The Archman is clearly competent in this kind of work. Perhaps it is the heavy blood loss or the anaesthetic substance in her system, but this is the first time she is truly okay leaving her life in his hands.

CHAPTER Two

A CAREFUL TENDING

A spray of seawater mists the air as Kinsley's battleship cuts through the restless ocean waves. The crew of officers moves about monotonously, as they have set their course and have yet to receive any further orders.

On the upper deck, Kinsley is looking out past the stern of the ship. His hands are on the wooden banister, his elbows are locked firmly, and his head is slouched over. It is a posture that appears to have quickly become his default ever since the ship's abrupt departure a few days ago.

A few higher-ranking officers pace about the upper deck, caught in an unfamiliar state of ambiguity from the lack of authority. They have managed to keep things running effectively enough without Kinsley's command, but they do so with chronic hesitancy.

"Should we..." One of the members of the crew turns to a fellow officer, both of whom are looking across the upper deck towards Kinsley. The fellow officer shrugs and does not reply.

Though Kinsley is standing just a few feet from them, he seems almost completely absent. He might as well be a statue they brought along for aesthetic purposes. The illusion is quickly broken, however, as Kinsley brings a closed fist down onto the banister, drawing the attention of everyone on the upper deck. There is a blistering frown across his brow, tensing every single muscle in his face with a seething contortion. It looks as though he is about to say something, but he remains completely quiet.

He suddenly turns around, causing the unwitting spectators around him to quickly avert their gaze and go back to whatever they were doing to keep themselves looking busy.

"Get me ink and paper." Kinsley walks towards the first mate, possessed by a fresh sense of obstinacy.

"Ah, yes Sir!" The first mate gives a brief salute and rushes down the stairs of the upper deck. Ordinarily he would delegate such a menial task to a deckhand, but he wants to make sure this duty is done to perfection.

Kinsley stands beside the officer at the steering wheel, neither of them looking at one another.

"How's our course been?" Kinsley asks gruffly.

"Excellent, no delays thus far." The officer is relieved that he has good news to report.

Kinsley does not acknowledge the officer's response. He simply extracts the information from his words and discards the rest of the unnecessary noise. He brings a hand to his chin, already starting to compose the letter he plans to write in his head.

The silent tension sets back in, and all the officers wait on pins and needles for Kinsley's next unpredictable action. It is going to be a long trip back.

THE DIM LAMPLIGHT OF THE ARCHMAN'S BEDROOM WARDS off the natural cloistering darkness of the space, providing just enough light to illuminate the pages of the book Eira has in her lap.

She is sitting up against the headboard of the bed with the blankets pulled up to her waist. Usually she would have her legs bent so that whatever reading material she had could be rested against her thighs, but the position is much too uncomfortable in her current state.

She adjusts the collar around her neck slightly, as she typically does every hour or so, to keep it from chafing the same portion of skin all the time.

There is a light knocking at the door, pulling Eira's attention up from the thick hardcover book and towards the closed door.

"Come in," she calls, loudly enough to be heard on the other side of the door. The words feel somewhat unnatural coming from her mouth. It has been a while since she has had had to exercise common courtesy, especially since she never expected to employ it in the Archman's company.

The door opens and the Archman enters, accompanied by a deluge of sunlight at his back. Eira shields the glaring light from her eyes, which are calibrated to the room's darkness. It really does not make sense to have a room completely closed off from the sun and lit instead by several lamps. However, it is clearly designed to accommodate the Archman's distasteful relationship with the sun.

"Since when do you knock before entering?" Eira asks, with a taunting angle to her words.

"Since I was born, I suppose. It's in my nature." The Archman removes his hood and walks over to Eira, carrying two items with him: a wooden board and one of his glass jars.

"Why now, though?"

"This is your room for now." He sets the glass jar down on the bedside table next to Eira and takes a seat on the end of the bed.

"So...?" Eira is not exactly following the Archman's logic.

"So, before entering someone else's room, you receive permission."

"How courteous," Eira says with a slight jeer, though she realises that what she is mocking is indeed quite courteous. It just does not make sense, coming from the Archman.

The Archman hands the wooden board to her. She sets her book aside to receive it. There are pieces of raw fish laid out across the piece of glossy wood, cut into even bite-sized slices, and sprinkled with flakes of sea salt. It is a considerable step up from the slabs of fresh fish she had become accustomed to eating recently, looking almost like a refined culinary creation one might serve to esteemed guests.

"Thanks." Eira tries not to sound as surprised as she is. At its core, the dish is still just fish and salt, but more effort and time have been put into it than usual.

"Oh, right..." The Archman reaches into the pockets of his pants and pulls out two pieces of dried meat, which he sets on the bedside table, next to the jar of water.

"Where did you get that?" Eira asks pensively, part of her heavily suspecting that it is human meat.

"I searched that pirate ship for food. This was all they had, though."

"The one you were going to set ablaze?" Eira clarifies, her diction lacking somewhat, as her mouth is occupied with eating fish.

"That was the plan, but it would've been a waste of time. Also didn't want to draw any more attention with the smoke," the Archman explains.

"Right..." Eira nods, keeping her words to a minimum.

"How's the wound?" The Archman scooches closer to Eira, pulling the blankets back from her waist.

"Oh...better, I guess." Eira is a bit startled by the sudden gesture, setting the wooden board aside to keep it out of the way. She is not sure why he even bothered asking if he was just going to check anyway.

"Any pain?" The Archman takes the hem of Eira's shirt, a plain white cotton pullover which is much too big for her, and lifts it up her midriff.

"A bit, but it's manageable." Eira finds it a bit jarring having the Archman handling her so casually, but the medical demeanour with which he approaches her helps to dismiss her reservations. He had just had his hands inside her guts a few days ago, so this is arguably much tamer in comparison.

The Archman analyses the scarred lesion on the right of her abdomen, which is only partially healed. The skin is still severely discoloured around the stitched puncture point.

Eira takes the hem of her shirt from him and holds it up for him. As she sits there, she finds herself wondering what might happen if she were just to lift the shirt off herself completely.

Eira dodges the strange question and pushes it to the back of her mind.

The Archman looks at the wound with his usual keen focus, lightly touching the skin around the stitches. The pressure aches a little bit, but it is somewhat comforting at the same time.

He pulls away and goes to his belt, forging through one of its many compartments in search of something. It is at this moment that Eira notices he had changed back into his ordinary attire: long-sleeved shirt, black cloak, and dark pants. She is not sure why, but she had gotten used to seeing him in his sleek combat ensemble, even though he had only worn it for a single day.

The Archman pulls a circular metal container out of his belt and twists the top off to reveal a translucent gel-like substance within. He removes his leather gloves and dips two fingers into the gel, then shifts his focus back to Eira.

Eira watches silently as he applies the gel to the scarred area of her stomach with his two fingers.

"Ah—" Eira quips, as the coagulated substance stings ever so slightly.

"Sorry," the Archman utters, not stopping his fingers for even a moment. "It'll get infected if I don't."

"I could do this, you know," Eira comments, though she knows that doing it herself will not make it sting any less.

"I'm sure you can, princess." The Archman nods, the corner of his mouth lifting into a faint smile. He finishes rubbing the gel on and around the wound, then closes the container and returns it to his belt.

Eira continues sitting still, holding up the hem of her shirt. There is a pause as he lifts his gaze to meet hers.

"You can lower your shirt now."

"Oh…" Eira sheepishly pulls her shirt down.

"Or not, be my guest." The Archman's smile turns to more of a smirk.

"So I'm your guest now?" Eira raises her eyebrow, engaging with him on his level of slyness. "Can we take this off, then?" She pulls at the collar on her neck.

"Mmm…no." The Archman runs a hand through his silver locks before he shuts her down playfully. He goes back to his belt and retrieves another item from the many compartments. It seems like absolutely everything he could possibly need is kept around his waist.

"I have something for you." He reaches out a closed hand, offering its contents to Eira. She opens her palm under his hand, and he drops a small metal ball into her possession.

Eira lifts the metal ball up to her eyes so that she can inspect it closer. It is a musket ball, one which has already been discharged. She is unsure what could possibly be significant about such a common item, until she realises what makes this one special.

"Is this…" She looks at the Archman, answering her own question as she asks it.

"I wasn't sure, but I thought it might have some sentimental value to you." The Archman shrugs, his tone suggesting that he is only half serious.

"Thanks…I suppose." Eira giggles lightly, looking at the musket ball in her palm. It is such an eclectic gift—one she surely never expected to receive at any point in her life.

"I'm no expert on marriage rituals or anything of that sort, but it seems like a strange custom for the groom to shoot the bride in the stomach." He crosses his arms and postulates with a satirical bent.

For the first time since being taken captive, Eira laughs with genuine jovialness. "Yes, I suspect it's a Catholic practice."

"Ah of course, I remember that famous passage. Ephesians 5:25: 'Husbands, love your wives, even as Christ also loved the church, and gave himself for her.'" He continues, "Then shot her in the gut." Both Eira and the Archman chuckle.

"I'm going to enjoy bringing up the fact he shot me every time one of my own shortcomings arises." Eira smiles and nods.

"Sounds like a flawless union to me." The Archman heckles with a spritely energy.

"Far from it." Eira lies back and sighs. The topic of her espousal to Kinsley seems to quickly lower her spirits, no matter how much humour could be derived from it.

"This was only my second time meeting him, you know. The first time was at some ball a year ago, and I can't even recall what we said to each other. He spoke with my mother after the fact and they arranged everything. I hardly remembered what he looked like until recently."

"You don't say. I would generally wait until I was better acquainted with someone before shooting them." The Archman chortles to himself.

"You certainly didn't bother to properly acquaint yourself with me when you tried to eat me," Eira teases light-heartedly.

"Well, you're an exception." The Archman stands up from the bed, putting his hood back over his head as he prepares to leave.

"Stay hydrated." He points to the jar of water on Eira's bedside table before making his way out the door.

Eira looks at the transparent container with the transparent liquid inside. She takes it off the table and brings it to her lips, downing almost half of it in one drink. She clearly did not realise how thirsty she had been getting.

THE ARCHMAN WALKS THROUGH THE DIM CORRIDORS below decks, carrying several medium-sized rags with him under one arm, and holding a bucket of soapy water in one hand. He opens the door to the room which acts as the designated slaughterhouse and ignites several of the lamps located around the small space.

He looks at the steel table in the centre of the room, which is still covered with stale blood from the hasty procedure from a few days prior. He approaches the sanguinary scene slowly, not in any particular rush to begin cleaning up. It is a task he has been putting off for some time now, but it has to get done at some point.

He looks down at the floorboards beneath his feet, which are lightly stained with blood that has dripped off the table. He dunks the rags in the bucket and starts mopping up the dried blood from the hard metal surface. He looks at the odd texture of the gore as he towels it up with the rags, soaking them intermittently in the bucket of water to clean them.

He tries to keep his focus on cleaning, but the blood captivates his attention with a visceral attraction, almost as if it were a puddle of gold flakes in the hands of an ambitious prospector. He runs two of his fingers through the dried blood, coating them in specks of red haemoglobin.

He stares at the vital fluid with increasing fixation, until a primordial impulse overtakes him, causing him to run his tongue along his fingers, gathering as much of the blood as he can into his mouth.

He stands stock still for several seconds, simply allowing the savoury experience to wash over him. Suddenly, he grabs the steel table with his hands and holds onto it with a vicious grip. He grits his teeth as he forcibly snaps himself out of his deluded state, wrestling himself back under control.

It tasted much better than he thought it would.

CHAPTER Three

A PARTICULAR STUDY

Eira sits in bed, reading under the warm light of the lamps. Her wound has healed enough to let her bend her legs at right angles to rest the hardcover book on her thighs. She brings a hand to her mouth and lets out a silent yawn. It is clearly born of ennui rather than fatigue as lately all she has been doing is sleeping and reading in order to recover.

She looks down at the book, which is written entirely in ancient Latin. Eira has a rudimentary grasp of the language, but that is not where the challenge really lies. What confounds her most is the cryptic speech and scientific jargon that fill the pages. It is a textbook of some kind, though she can hardly grasp what exactly it is meant to instruct. She has not really absorbed any information whatsoever from the pages, which is quite something, considering her insatiable appetite for knowledge.

Eira closes the book and sets it aside. Prompted by the thought of her appetite, she looks over at her bedside table where she sees an empty wooden cutting board and a vacant glass jar. She is not actually hungry, she just needs something to occupy her.

In a flash of inquisitive curiosity, Eira looks down at the chain secured to the collar around her neck. She pulls the chain up onto the bed, letting the slack pile up beside her. As she arrives at the end of the chain, she is perplexed to see the final link in her hand.

The Archman must have forgotten to lock it to the bed after escorting her to and from the latrine or, perhaps, he had just decided against locking it back up, assuming Eira would stay put regardless.

Either way, she jumps at the opportunity, gathers up the slack in her hands, and slips out of bed, careful not to open her wound in the process. She is wearing a nightgown which comes down to her ankles. The garment is in desperate need of laundering after several days and nights in bed.

Eira walks to the end of the bedroom and opens the door slowly so her eyes can adjust to the light. She steps out onto the main deck, letting the sunlight warm her skin and spirit. She is aware she is going against the Archman's wishes, but the fresh air is well worth it.

If the Archman were to find her wandering about, he would surely be irritated and send her back to the bedroom. If she sought him out specifically, he would likely be less bothered, or so Eira reasoned to herself. She needs to find a reasonable reason to seek him out, though.

She goes back into the bedroom and retrieves the hardcover book from the bed, bringing it along with her, chain in one arm, book in the other. She is unsure he will buy her excuse, but it is at least worth the attempt.

She makes her way below decks, climbing down the first set of stairs to the landing. She looks down the corridor to her left and opts to search this area first.

She peeks inside the massive walk-in closet and quickly discerns that he is not there. She goes to the next door down the corridor, which is locked shut. This is the only door which has a lock on it, which attracts Eira's attention much more than she wishes it did.

She forces herself to ignore the door and moves on to the next one. She puts her ear against the door before opening it. She is able to hear a noise coming from behind it: it is some kind of activity or liveliness.

Eira pushes the door open with her shoulder, as both her hands are occupied. She finds herself in a large study, every inch of wall covered by bookshelves, and every inch of bookshelf occupied with books.

"You shouldn't be walking." Eira snaps her attention forwards to the end of the study, where the Archman is sitting behind a wide desk. She is surprised that she had not noticed him at first—his natural stillness must have fooled her into thinking he was some large portrait.

What might have additionally contributed to this visual oversight is the pair of spectacles resting on the bridge of the Archman's nose. It is a deeply mystifying sight, as he seems like the last person who would don some kind of eyewear. In spite of this, they fit his face perfectly, adding an element of sophistication and intelligence to his character. If Eira was not already aware of his capacity for cruelty, her first impression would be that of a reputable gentleman.

His professor-like ambience is further contrasted by a glass container resting on the desk, half-full of a red liquid. It only takes Eira a moment to realise what that scarlet elixir is.

"I'm doing quite alright, thanks," Eira responds quickly, realising that she has been staring at the Archman for several seconds without replying.

The Archman removes his glasses and sets them aside and then gets up from his desk. Eira feels a twinge of disappointment, as she had not finished observing him in his spectacled state.

"Regardless, I trust you have good reason for coming here." The Archman wipes a few lingering drops of blood from his lips as he walks over to Eira and takes the bundle of chains from her hands. She immediately surrenders the mass of metal links to him, relieved not to be lugging the weight around anymore.

"I'm done with this." Eira holds up the hardcover book, offering it to the Archman.

"You're finished reading it?" He takes the book from her.

"No, but I'm done with it."

The Archman exhales and walks over to one of the bookshelves and returns the book to a single empty spot.

"Not fond of the chemical sciences?"

"I'll let you know once I can understand what they're about." Eira shrugs.

"Well, if that doesn't suit your tastes, then I doubt there is much else here that will." The Archman scans the bookshelves, squinting slightly to read the titles across the many spines.

"You don't have anything you read for pleasure?"

"If you mean literature or anything of that sort, then no, I'm afraid not."

"None at all?" Eira looks around the study, simultaneously amazed and discouraged by the wealth of information in her surroundings.

"It's not a priority."

"That's disappointing." Eira sighs.

"I don't recall asking for your input," the Archman retorts gruffly.

"Where did you even find all these?" Eira probes, walking up beside the Archman to survey the same books as him.

"I wrote them."

"You mean...all of them?" Eira looks around at the vast collection of books in her wake, trying to estimate how many hundreds of thousands of hours it would take to fill so many pages.

"So...you never opted to write any fiction?" Eira looks up to the Archman, trying to conceal her astonishment.

"Again, it's not a priority."

"Why not? Everyone loves a good story," Eira enquires further.

"My function is the deconstruction and comprehension of all material phenomena. I don't have any stories worth telling."

"Somehow I doubt that."

The Archman looks down at Eira, waiting for her to explain herself.

"You're centuries old, aren't you?"

"Millennia," the Archman corrects.

"My point exactly. You mean to tell me that in the hundreds of lifetimes you've lived, you don't have a single story worth telling?"

"Nothing anyone would want to hear." The Archman tries to brush off Eira's persistence, but she is not so easily dissuaded.

"How do you know no one wants to hear them if you never tell them?" Eira argues.

The Archman looks down at her, his expression frozen completely still in the face of her rhetoric. He backtracks quickly to form a rebuttal.

"What are you doing here, again?" He narrows his vermillion eyes on her with a debilitating energy.

"You mean in this room or my place in the greater universe?" Eira deflects humbly.

"You know damn well what I mean." The Archman's cold demeanour is unable to completely stifle the chortle which escapes his mouth.

"Well, I was hoping for some more enjoyable reading material, but I suppose that won't be happening." Eira sighs with exaggerated disappointment.

The Archman turns around and searches through the bookshelves on the other side of the room. "If it's an exciting reading experience you're after..."— he pulls a single book out of the shelf and dusts it off before handing it to Eira—"...then perhaps you'd like this."

Eira looks at the front cover, which presents a series of geometric patterns that does not help to identify the contents of the book at all. Eira fans through the pages, until she sees a pencil illustration which catches her attention. She opens the page up to reveal a large phallic image, which takes up the majority of the page. Her eyes immediately widen, completely fixated on the highly detailed sketch. She has an impulse to slam the book shut, but an even deeper impulse compels her to keep it open.

"What exactly gave you the impression this would interest me?" Eira drags her attention away from the page, up to the Archman.

"I know how fond humans are of their reproductive systems." The Archman has a devious smirk across his face.

"That doesn't apply to all of us, you know," Eira retorts.

"If you don't want it, I'll take it back." The Archman holds out a hand, offering to reclaim the book from her.

Eira looks back to the book in her hands, caught in a position where she cannot possibly win. She resigns herself with as much dignity as she can, closes the book, and puts it under her arm.

"No, it will suffice." She exhales with a heavy exasperation, trying to make it clear that the book is a final option which she is not particularly attached to, regardless of whether that is true or not.

"If you say so, princess." The Archman chuckles as he hands the bundle of chains to her as she starts moving towards the door.

Before passing through the doorway, Eira turns back towards the Archman.

"I'm not a princess, you know."

"Oh? What should I call you, then?" The Archman playfully raises an eyebrow.

"My name's Eira. Maybe try that."

"Eira. Alright then." The Archman nods. "Now get back to bed."

Eira walks back up to the main deck towards the bedroom beneath the upper deck. Before she re-enters the cave-like space, she waits outside, soaking up a couple more lingering rays of sunlight.

As she turns to open the bedroom door, she sees something out of the corner of her eye. She looks across the deck and past the bow of the boat, out to the rippling waters ahead.

A small, unsuspecting vessel is coming towards the Archman's ship. There are no noticeable insignias or other identifying characteristics to the ship, just plain, off-white sails and a hull composed of sea-aged wood. The first impression is that of some humble fishing boat and, as it draws nearer, that impression becomes more and more evident to Eira.

The small watercraft makes its way closer to the Archman's ship, moving gently with the timid afternoon winds. It approaches on the port side of the Archman's ship, passing by at a leisurely pace, only a few feet separating the two vessels from one another.

Eira walks slowly to the edge of the deck, looking down over the banister at the small watercraft as it passes by. She finds herself in a perplexing condition, neither relieved nor concerned by the foreign watercraft.

A solitary sailor is on the deck of his fishing boat, tending to the rigging of his modest vessel. He spots Eira looking down at him and removes his wide-brimmed sun hat to look up and return the gaze.

"Afternoon, ma'am." The sailor raises a hand, a kind of amicable gesture he has reserved specifically for greeting strangers and close companions who tend to make him uncomfortable.

"Afternoon." Eira reciprocates the gesture with a nod. She would have given a wave in return, if not for her hands being both heavily occupied.

"Been a stellar week, hasn't it? Can't remember the last time it rained." The sailor indicates up to the sky with his sun hat.

"Quite. Hardly a cloud in the sky." Eira agrees, nodding her head once more. It has not really been a great week for her, recovering from a nearly fatal gut wound, but she decides against mentioning that detail.

"Well, you have a good one, then." The sailor's ship has started to make its way past the Archman's, creating a natural end to the conversation.

"Thanks, you too." Eira nods for a third time. She feels she can only perform the gesture a few more times before it will become overused.

Fortunately, she does not have to, as the sailor's ship drifts away from her at the same steady pace it arrived at. Eira and the sailor part and go their separate ways.

Eira steps away from the banister of the ship, holding the bundle of chains and book in her arms. She walks back towards the bedroom in a dazed state, trying to make sense of herself. She had just been presented with a prime opportunity to escape; she could have easily called out to the sailor and leapt overboard into his custody, and the Archman would have been none the wiser. It was an occasion that would surely never present itself again, and yet she let it slip right through her fingers.

She feels like she is in a trance, as if she is not in charge of her speech and action— like there is something beyond herself now compelling her being. Perhaps the wound to her stomach caused all the autonomy and rationality to leak out of her abdomen. It is a jarring sensation and yet does not inspire any kind of anxiety or worry.

As she slips back into the darkness of the bedroom, Eira figures that she can learn to live with this new feeling.

CHAPTER

Four

A SOMATIC FANTASY

Kinsley sits at the desk in his spacious but cramped office. Standing before him is a decently dressed man, who is clearly a few income levels below Kinsley. The man is wearing some kind of governmental attire, though it is not much to be impressed by, especially contrasted with the costly decor of Kinsley's office. The man has a thin wood board in his grasp, with several papers resting precariously upon it. They are held down only by the man's left hand; his other hand is tightly gripping a quill.

"And where was this person last seen?" the man asks.

"About forty miles off the western coast. I don't have the exact coordinates," Kinsley replies, wringing his hands slightly together to occupy himself.

"Any defining features he can be identified by?" The man scrawls on the paper before him as he asks his next question.

Kinsley reaches into the pocket of his elegant jacket, drawing out a folded piece of paper. He extends it to the man, who sets his wooden board down to receive it. He unfolds it, revealing a detailed drawing of the Archman, done with preliminary sketches and traced over carefully with ink. There was evidently much effort placed into the drawing.

"Ah...that helps." The man nods, not expecting such an exact characterisation. "What did you say his name was again?"

"The Archman. He has no real name." Kinsley's features tense as he speaks the Archman's title.

"Oh...pardon?" the man says with a perplexed tone.

"The Archman? I'm sure you've heard the fables."

"Yes, I have, but..." The man looks back and forth between Kinsley and the drawing of the Archman, as if the clarity he seeks exists in either place. "Forgive my asking, Commodore, but this isn't some kind of wild goose chase, is it?"

Kinsley glares at the man with an expression that is quickly approaching a livid quality. "I met him myself. We crossed blades. Do you mean to call me a liar?"

The man's posture tightens, along with his grip on the quill. "Certainly not, Sir...my apologies." The man folds and pockets the drawing and picks his wooden board back up, hoping to quickly change the subject.

"And how much for his capture?"

"Three thousand pounds. Twice that if they bring him in alive."

The man makes some quick scrawls on the papers before him, sacrificing legibility for speed, as he is eager to have the interaction with Kinsley over with. He wipes the tip of the quill on a handkerchief dedicated to that specific purpose, pockets the two implements, and walks to the exit.

"We'll write to you when the order goes through," he says with a small bow, turning and walking away in the same motion. As the man exits through the heavy office doors, he crosses paths with Normond, who is moving at a similarly hurried pace.

Normand pushes past the man as though he were one of the doors obstructing his course, walks briskly into the office, and treks right up to Kinsley.

"Kinsley! Sir! I heard what happened!" Normand removes his hat respectfully as he approaches the large desk. "Are you alright?!"

"Been better, frankly." Kinsley stands up from his desk in a brusque manner. "I very nearly had him. He just barely slipped my grasp."

"He certainly seems to be the elusive type." Normand nods in accord. He suddenly remembers a concern which he had set aside previously. "And what of Miss Pryce?"

Kinsley pauses for an extended moment, his face very slowly morphing into a bitter sneer.

"I believe she's alive...but she's being held hostage by that wretch." Kinsley decides to omit certain details about how the conflict ended.

"Dear God..." Normand grips his hat in his hands, scrunching the brim between his fingers nervously.

"Now that you're back, we can proceed further." Kinsley steps out from around his desk, straightening his jacket as he prepares to leave.

"Proceed in what manner?" Normand returns his hat to his head, subtly mimicking Kinsley's actions.

"We're going to speak with Sir Wilcox."

A murky abstractness surrounds Eira's consciousness as her body rests in a dense slumber. From the nothingness that envelops her, indiscriminate pieces of stimulus flash briefly into existence, fading momentarily in and out of her perception. At first they are just scraps of sensory experience gathered from random points in her daily routines: still images, auditory sounds, aromatic moments, tactile feelings, and savoury instances.

From the cacophony of stimulants rushing through her head, a few select pieces stick to her consciousness. From these shreds of reality, an unobserved part of Eira's mind takes over, filling in the empty spaces between the scraps of actuality to create an experience more suited to her fantasy.

Eira now finds herself embraced by a peculiar mix of warmth and coldness, causing her sleeping body to shiver and relax. Though she can feel the distinct difference in temperature, it is clear to her that both the heat and coldness come from the same source. The source closes itself around Eira, holding to her tightly. Eira brings her arms around this fount of opposing heat and embraces it back. There is little of this climatic force for her to understand other than the fact that it has an intimate purity to it.

Both Eira and the sensory entity hug one another with a deepening proximity, as if they are trying to make as much contact with one another as possible.

Eira feels her skin start to tingle with a gentle prickling. It quickly spreads out across her entire corporeal form, wrapping her in a blanket of sizzling energy. Eira breaths in and feels the vibrational force spread into her lungs, resonating outward into all the muscles and organs in her upper body.

As if to match this sensation with an equal but opposite force, the entity starts to slowly enter Eira from between her legs, spreading the tingling energy throughout her lower body.

Eira's body tenses then relaxes, both in her physical anatomy and its metaphysical counterpart. The tingling sensation grows in strength and density as the entity impels itself deeper inside her, guiding the energy up to her head. As the tingle envelops and permeates her cranium, it slowly develops into a blissful hum, dulling all her senses with an almost euphoric delight.

She pulls the entity closer, inviting it deeper inside her. Its existence feels so foreign to her, and yet it meshes perfectly with her body. She looks up at it and tries to observe it as best she can with her hazy eyesight. She stares long and hard but can only make out the faintest of details. The entity has a vague anatomy which approximates that of a human person, but with much less-defined borders.

For a brief second she can detect a flash of silver brushing across her face. She focuses intently on where it came from, trying to find any more identifying features. She stares in the direction the silver flashes originated from, and notices that it came from the figure's head, or what resembles the general impression of a head. As she narrows her gaze, she is just barely able to make out four or five faint lines imprinted on the entity's face. Upon closer inspection, Eira realises they are scars.

Now completely enraptured by the entity's presence, she lifts a hand and brushes aside the flashes of silver from between herself and the entity. She is both shocked and amazed to find herself met with a pair of small blood-red orbs, which seem to reflect her gaze right back to her.

Before she can witness anything more, a jarring sound from the outside world pulls her out of her dream, back into the harsh reality of material life.

Eira sits up in her bed, blinking several times as she crosses the awkward threshold between sleep and wakefulness. Her whole body is covered in a damp sweat, causing her nightgown to cling all over her. It may just be her imagination, but it feels like there is significantly more wetness around her lower body than before, especially between her thighs.

There is a quick but loud knock on the door of the bedroom. It is the same sound which had abruptly roused her from her slumber.

"Just a moment!" Eira pulls herself out of bed, pushing her knotted hair out of her face. It is not until she is standing up, rubbing the sleep out of her eyes that she realises she is not at home in her bed. When she discovers that she is in the Archman's bedroom, she is not particularly disturbed or upset, mostly just discombobulated. She looks around the dark room, trying to figure out why she got up out of bed so hastily.

The impulse to rise quickly and make herself presentable is one that had been worked into her many times over throughout her youth, but in this circumstance it serves little purpose. She has no means or reason to tend to her appearance in front of the Archman. Considering that he has already witnessed her with her guts opened up, it would be hard to present herself in an even more unappealing light. Part of her wishes there would be some opportunity to make herself tidy and groomed, since the Archman has only ever seen her in a dishevelled, repugnant state.

"Oh—come in!" Eira snaps her attention to the door, realising that she has been standing still with her thoughts for several long seconds.

The Archman opens the door and takes a step into the bedroom. He and Eira lock eyes for a moment, the contact lasting half a beat longer than it typically does. His gaze trails down Eira's body, then back up to her face as he analyses her appearance. He notes that she is much sweatier than usual.

"Sleep well?" The Archman poses the question with a genuine curiosity, as opposed to the standard indifference with which the question is often asked.

"Uh..." Eira replays the night in her head, her attention centring on the strange dream she experienced. It was a most peculiar dream for her, since most of the nocturnal hallucinations throughout her life tended to conjure specific recognisable images or tangible narratives instead of random, abstract sensations.

"It was fine," Eira responds plainly. It would have been much too complicated to try and explain what her dream entailed, and she is not particularly eager to share it in the first place.

"Good, you'll need the energy today." The Archman walks over to the bed and gathers up the chain secured to Eira's collar, coiling it up into a uniform ring.

"I will?" Eira follows the Archman outside of the bedroom, into the glaring midnoon sunlight. She is not sure what kind of exertion is going to be expected of her. It has been quite a while since she has needed to do any kind of physical labour.

As they step out onto the main deck, Eira immediately notices something out of the ordinary about the view in front of them. They are quickly approaching the mainland, which stretches out across them at imperceptible lengths on either side. They are only a few miles from the shore.

Eira keeps her eyes glued to the approaching shoreline as she follows the Archman up the stairs to the upper deck. The ship appears to be headed for some kind of large port which Eira is entirely unfamiliar with, not that she is any kind of expert on naval topography to begin with.

"Where are we going?" Eira turns to the Archman as they arrive behind the steering wheel.

"Econridge. If memory serves me, it's a port outside the jurisdiction of the Royal Navy. Hopefully that's still the case." The Archman looks out past the bow of the ship to the port in the approaching distance.

"You're planning on hiding here?" Eira tries to piece together the Archman's plan from the minute bits of information she has available.

"No, I don't think hiding will be possible anymore. Evidently that husband of yours is quite tenacious."

"He's not my—"

"Right, fiancé. Whatever. The point is, I doubt hiding from him is a viable option. We're here to hire some defence."

"Defence?" Eira has a general idea of what the Archman is suggesting but desires more clarity.

"There's plenty of privateers and mercenaries for hire who can grant some protection until we're out of the Royal Navy's reach. Though if luck is on my side, there will be a certain group of privateers available."

"Who's that?"

"The Raeburn family is an infamous band of pirates. They have a small fleet under their command. I met one of them a while back, so perhaps there is an old connection to rekindle," the Archman says, postulating. He raises a hand to his chin as another consideration comes across his mind. “Mind you, that was sixty years ago...he’s most certainly dead by now.”

Eira nods as the Archman lays out his objective.

“What do you need me for, then?” she enquires.

“Nothing. You’re simply too crafty to be left alone for too long.” The Archman chortles to himself, one of his white fangs briefly flashing into view out of the corner of his mouth.

“How flattering,” Eira quips, smiling with exaggerated pride.

This was probably the most she has heard him speak, a stark contrast to his usual monosyllabic vocabulary. She is not sure why, but it puts her in a pleasant mood.

CHAPTER Five

A TENSE RECRUITMENT, PART 1

The Archman pulls on a pair of oars, rowing a small dinghy through the water to the busy harbour. Eira sits across from him, carrying the slackened chain attached to her collar. She looks around at the surrounding harbour, a large crescent-shaped beachfront with a few shabby docks built along the shoreline. Though it is a marina notorious for hosting people of the criminal variety, there is still a feel of orderly regulation and respectability. Nearly forty other ships of various sizes and purposes are anchored down in the harbour, floating unoccupied in the calm water. The Archman's ship stands out from the rest quite prominently, both in its sheer magnitude and its technologically advanced rigging.

They approach one of the small wooden docks, which has a couple of dinghies already resting in place. Just as with the ships they belong to, the small boats come in a variety of sizes and makes. Some of them are visibly older and worn down, while others are either newly built or recently refurbished.

The Archman pulls the oars into the dinghy as it floats up beside the dock. He steps out and takes a coil of rope from the small watercraft, lashing it to a nearby post.

Eira stands up in the boat, careful not to make any sudden movements. She looks for a spot to place her hand in order to steady herself so she can exit. She finds the Archman's conveniently outstretched hand and takes it as he pulls her up onto the dock.

The Archman takes the bundle of chains from Eira and makes his way along the dock. Eira follows beside him as they make their way towards the sprawling village of Econridge, which wraps itself around the harbour, acting more as an extension of the port rather than its own solitary destination.

As Eira and the Archman walk into the village, it becomes clear that it could not exist without the harbour, as almost every other person they walk by has some kind of marine-related occupation.

The Archman tugs at the hood over his head and pulls it partially over his face to disguise himself from the people around them. Eira rarely flourishes in public settings, but after several weeks of being confined to the Archman's ship, she finds herself rejuvenated from being in the proximity of so many people.

Eira feels a yank on her collar, drawing her attention towards the Archman, who is now several steps ahead of her, evidently irked by her lackadaisical pace.

"We're not tourists. Save the sightseeing for another time."

"I didn't realise we were in such a rush," Eira comments snarkily as she quickens her pace to catch up with the Archman.

"The less time we spend here the better."

Eira pays more attention so as not to fall behind; she walks in parallel with the Archman. It takes considerable effort on her part, since his strides are so much longer than hers. As they walk along, Eira starts to notice they are getting glances from the occasional person walking by. From an outsider's perspective, it is certainly an odd sight, seeing a woman being led along on a leash like some kind of mutt.

Despite the appearance, however, Eira does not really feel like any kind of domesticated animal, though she certainly does not feel like she has the level of dignity to which the average person is due.

"This should be it." The Archman stops before a large inn that stands three stories tall, a significantly larger stature than most of the surrounding buildings.

"Where are we?" Eira looks up to survey the structure. It is an aged building: the stonework has eroded from nearly a century of exposure to the abrasive sea air.

"Last I checked, the Raeburns own this property. It's where we're most likely to find them."

Standing perfectly still, the Archman stares at the faded wooden front door of the inn with a disgruntled look about him. He is wrestling with some kind of personal gridlock that results in a frustrated mood, though it is unclear exactly what is frustrating him. He turns towards Eira, his irritation visibly contained.

"I need you to do something."

Eira is surprised to hear those words come from the Archman's mouth, and he has not even explained what he needs her to do yet. The very fact of him requesting assistance for any task is astonishing enough.

"Okay," Eira says hesitantly, not wanting to fully agree to anything just yet.

"Go inside and find whoever owns the place, then bring them out to me," the Archman instructs clearly, as if Eira has already agreed to the assignment.

"Why don't you just—"

"That's not an option. Can you do it?"

Eira pauses for a moment, looks to the door, and then back at the Archman.

"Sure, I think so."

"Keep your head down and be quick about it," the Archman warns as he hands the bundle of chains to her.

Eira nods as she receives the bunch of metal links, then turns and opens the door. She walks in pensively.

The inside of the inn is teeming with a lively energy: upbeat string music is playing, food and alcohol are being consumed liberally, and there is a cacophony of conversations. It feels more like a tavern than an inn. Perhaps it acts as both.

A few stray eyes turn to Eira as she walks into the open room. Most of them trail off after a while, though a few promiscuous gazes linger on her. It is not immediately obvious who the owner of the property is. Eira had hoped that maybe there would be some affluent-looking person standing out from the common masses who looked indisputably like a landowner, but no such person can be found. Much to her discontent, she will have to speak with someone.

Eira's eyes land on a young man working behind a countertop. He is in the middle of polishing several mugs and glasses. He seems to be the best person to ask for information, as well as the least awkward individual to approach.

"Um, excuse me?" Eira walks up to the counter, pulling the attention of the bartender away from his glasses and mugs.

The two look at one another for a full second. The bartender analyses every aspect of Eira's appearance. She does not appear much different from the average patron, though the collar around her neck and the bundle of chains in her hands is certainly a perplexing feature.

"Can I help you?" the bartender asks politely. He usually greets guests with a curt "Whaddaya want?" but he makes an exception for pretty girls. Unless they are egregiously attractive, in which case he employs more abrasiveness than usual.

"Can you tell me who owns this place? Are they here?" Eira poses the questions as normally as she can, though the effort to appear normal only makes her stand out more.

"Sure, she's right over there." The bartender points across the room to a woman sitting alone at a table in the centre of the large room. She has her feet up on the empty table before her as she leans back in her chair, her arms crossed over her chest, and a leather cap covering the majority of her face.

"Oh, thank you."

Eira walks over to the woman at a slow pace, not sure of the proper way to approach someone sitting in such a peculiar manner. She certainly does not fit the image in Eira's mind of an esteemed property owner. The woman's clothes would have, at one point, been considered elegant and expensive, but after decades of being handed down and swapped around, the clothes are well past their prime. She is wearing the jacket from an old naval uniform. The sleeves have been cut off, turning it into more of a vest. The fabric is full of runs and small tears, and the gold embroidery is heavily faded. Below that is a simple pair of comfortable cloth pants held up with a thick black belt, which looks to be holding a flintlock pistol. Her feet are clad in a pair of brown leather boots, which come halfway up her shins. Her long golden hair, which hangs loose across the back of her chair, is the only thing about her appearance which really resembles Eira's image of a respectable landowner. Unlike the woman's unkempt clothing, her hair is in nearly perfect condition.

Eira walks up beside the woman so that she is standing about three feet away. She is not sure how to get her attention; she had expected the woman to simply notice her when she walked up, but clearly that has not happened. Eira leans in to inspect the woman further, then pulls back when she hears her snoring. It seems impossible for someone to sleep in such an unusual position, but clearly it is doable with enough practice.

"Pardon me...?" Eira speaks at a slightly softer tone than usual.

The woman does not respond at all and simply continues with her physics-defying nap.

Eira reaches a tentative hand out and taps the woman lightly on the shoulder. "Excuse m—"

The woman's cap tumbles off her head as she snaps awake within a split second. She grabs the wrist of Eira's outstretched arm with one hand as her other hand grabs the handle of her pistol. Eira freezes in place as the woman looks up at her with a deadly gaze. They connect for a tense moment, then the woman releases her grip on the pistol and Eira's wrist.

"*Sacrebleu!* You nearly scared the *bejesus* out of me." The woman exhales as she removes her feet from the table and sits upright.

"Oh...sorry." Eira apologises. Her heart is still racing from the woman's sudden movement. Eira is fortunate to have a relatively innocent appearance, as any shred of danger on her person would have surely inspired a more brutal impulse from the woman.

"I hope you have a good reason for waking me." The woman retrieves her cap from the floor, dusting it off before returning it to her head. "I was in the middle of a dream where I was making love with a prince."

"Oh..." Eira nods uncomfortably. She is not used to such blatant honesty. "Sorry..." she apologises again, just to be safe.

"Yeah, yeah. I know. You said that *déjà.* So what do you want?" The woman crosses her arms again; this appears to be a resting position for her.

Eira looks at the woman in stunned silence, still trying to process the person in front of her. There are so many odd things about her that Eira feels like she is talking to three people. As if her atypical wardrobe and unfiltered nature were not strange enough, Eira is still unable to wrap her head around the woman's dialect. Her accent is fundamentally English, but it has a heavy foreign sound to it which pops out every now and then with the sudden incorporation of French into her vocabulary. It sounds like an old habit passed down from previous generations, along with her golden hair and azure eyes.

"You...this is your inn, right?" Eira asks reluctantly.

"Yeah, it's mine. Mine and *mon frère*—my brother." The woman nods.

"My, uh, friend outside wishes to speak with you." Eira points towards the door.

"Sure, bring him over." The woman tucks her hair behind her ear and adjusts her cap.

"Actually, he...well, he can't."

"*Quoi?* What? Is he shy?" The woman raises an eyebrow, keeping her arms firmly crossed.

"Not quite, he's just...he's a bit odd." Eira tries to explain as best she can with the limited information she has.

"Is he handsome?" the woman asks, now raising both her eyebrows.

Eira stands in silence for what feels like the longest second of her life.

"Uh...yes, I suppose so." She is willing to say anything at this point to get the woman's assistance, but she is comfortable knowing that she is not lying.

"Alright then." The woman stands up from her chair and makes her way briskly towards the door. Eira, taken aback by how easily the woman cooperated, follows her to the doorway.

It feels like the woman is operating at a much more rapid pace than everything and everyone around her, Eira especially.

A TENSE RECRUITMENT, PART 2

The woman steps outside the inn with Eira in tow. The Archman is standing before them patiently. The woman looks up at him for a brief moment, simply to take in his presence.

"*Mon Dieu*, you weren't kidding." The woman turns to Eira, both her eyebrows raised in genuine amazement.

The Archman takes his own moment to observe the woman, noting specifically her golden locks and blue eyes. They are in direct contrast to the Archman's silver hair and crimson irises.

"Raeburn?" the Archman asks plainly.

"Oh, have we met before?" The woman turns back to the Archman, twirling her blond hair around one of her fingers.

"I doubt it. I knew your relative, though. Leonard Raeburn," the Archman says.

"You knew *grand-père* Leo?" The woman is astonished, trying to piece together how someone who knew a recent ancestor could look so young.

Eira stands by idly, her fingers fiddling with the bundle of chains in her grasp. She wishes she had something more to contribute to the conversation, but she cannot find any opportunity to step in.

"We met briefly." The Archman nods.

"*Vraiment...*" The woman scratches the back of her head, still gripped with fascination.

"*C'est toujours* a delight when old family friends pay a visit. Always a pleasure." She turns back towards the door, gesturing for the Archman to follow. "Let's go."

"May I come in?" The Archman stays perfectly still, not responding to the woman's gesture at all.

"Uh, of course. *Bien sûr,*" the woman states with confusion, seeing as it was already obvious that he could enter.

"You have to say it," the Archman demands.

"*Quoi?*" The woman looks at the Archman, her confusion growing deeper by the second.

"You have to say 'Come in,'" Eira points out, eager for the chance to interject.

"Okay...*entrez.*" The woman opens the door and indicates to the interior of the building with her head, swishing her golden hair inadvertently.

"*Merci,*" the Archman says courteously, walking inside.

Eira follows behind him, then the woman enters last, behind Eira.

"I'll take that back now." The Archman reaches out an open palm, requesting the bundle of chains from Eira.

"Oh, right." Eira returns the chains to the Archman.

"I have a table over there." The woman points to the table where she was napping earlier when Eira had approached her. Eira and the Archman follow her to the round wooden surface, pull up two chairs, and sit down to join her.

"I gotta know, *que fais-tu* to keep your skin so young?" The woman crosses her arms on the table and leans forward, admiring the Archman's complexion.

"I drink human blood," the Archman says with an indifferent curtness.

"Aha! *Fantastique*! Why didn't I think of that?" The woman laughs gleefully, reacting to a nonexistent humour from the Archman's words.

"Oh, *pardonnez-moi*, I nearly forgot." The woman says, offering her excuses as she extends her hand to the Archman for a handshake. "*Je m'appelle* Fiona. Pleasure meeting you."

"Likewise." The Archman takes Fiona's hand and shakes it as briefly as can be considered polite.

"What about you...?" Fiona pries with unabashed eagerness.

"That's not relevant," the Archman says dismissively.

"'Not relevant?' Hmm, I haven't heard that one before. Is it German?" Fiona smiles jubilantly.

"No." The Archman's expression seems to grow only more perfunctory the longer the interaction goes on.

"And how about you?" Fiona turns to Eira, leaning back off the table.

"Eira Pryce. Nice to meet you." Eira nods respectfully, a gesture to replace the handshake she was not offered.

"So you wanted to have a *parlé*?" Fiona turns to the Archman, leaning forwards once again.

"I'm looking to hire some protection from the navy," the Archman explains as simply as he can. "Last I checked, your family was notorious for thwarting the authorities."

"Hmm, that was *certainement* the case back in *grand-père* Leo's day. *Je dirai*, I will say, we're not quite as powerful as we were back then, but I'm sure we could still be of assistance."

Fiona plants both hands on the table and stands up suddenly, pushing her chair back by several feet. "Let me go get *mon frère;* we make all our big decisions together."

She walks away at her usual rapid pace, disappearing up a staircase to the upper floors.

"She seems nice." Eira turns to the Archman, filling the empty air before it inevitably gets overtaken by Fiona's energy once again.

"Don't be so easily swayed," he advises. "We're not here to hire likeable individuals."

Fiona returns into view, coming down the staircase at a significantly slower pace then she left. She would be operating at her typically swift stride, if she were not encumbered by a man who she is helping down the staircase. The cumbersome fellow looks to be the exact male equivalent of Fiona. He is sporting the same ragged clothing which at one point was considered fashionable, the same azure eyes, and the same golden blonde hair, cut short. There is a significant difference between the two of them, however: the man's demeanour is nowhere near as upbeat as Fiona's.

As they reach the bottom of the staircase and start making their way towards the table, it becomes clear that the man is not in good health. His breathing is shallow, his face flushed red, and, based on how much Fiona is supporting him, evidently lacks energy. His languished state could theoretically be the result of too much drinking, though he looks far too present and aware for that to be the case.

The Archman's eyes narrow on the man with an observational certainty as Fiona pulls up a chair for him to sit at the table.

"The hell you looking at?" The man locks eyes with the Archman, sending the cold glare right back at him.

"This is Eira and her *copain.*" Fiona gestures to the two of them as she speaks to the man, who is unable to find a comfortable position to sit in.

"This is *mon frère,* Jacob." Fiona reverses her gesture to the man and her speech to Eira and the Archman.

"*Mon Dieu!* I can introduce myself!" Jacob scoffs bitterly. In spite of his abrasive attitude, he is undoubtedly Fiona's blood relative.

"He knew *grand-père* Leo, apparently." Fiona ignores Jacob's acerbic tone, pointing back to the Archman.

Jacob's eyes widen with shock, his brusque energy dispersing for a moment as he is completely taken aback. He turns towards Fiona, his flushed face now devoid of all colour. "*C'est impossible.*"

"I thought so too. He looks much too young to be Leo's *ami.*" Fiona pokes at the Archman playfully with her elbow. Somehow she had managed to move around the table into his proximity without anyone noticing.

"But what is he doing here?" Jacob's initial shock has worn off, replaced with a new kind of harshness, one that is much more densely focused than before.

"He needs *protection* from the navy. He's here to hire us as his guards."

"Didn't it occur to you why he might need *protection*?" Jacob leans in towards Fiona, as if to close Eira and the Archman out of the conversation.

"*Non...*" Fiona responds honestly, growing nervous by Jacob's terse mood. She is used to dealing with him in his sickly state and can tell this particular behaviour has to do with something else.

"You don't remember who *grand-père* Leo said he once met? *Quelqu'un* who never aged?" The more Jacob's voice lowers in volume, the harsher it becomes.

Fiona's expression freezes with surprise as she suddenly realises what Jacob is referring to.

"*L'Archomme.* The Archman." Jacob turns to the Archman, proclaiming his title out loud, for everyone nearby to hear. Several pairs of eyes turn to their table, a few conversations dropping gradually out of the space.

"I had hoped that my infamy wouldn't prevent us from working together." The Archman speaks with his usual stolid demeanour.

"*Ordinairement*, that would be the case, but you've become quite the subject of interest lately," Jacob retorts.

"In what way?" The Archman probes, not surrendering any rhetorical ground.

"A bounty of *six mille*—six thousand—on your head." Jacob keeps his distance from the Archman, but his words reach right across the table to make up for the separation.

"So let me ask you. Why would I work with you..."—Jacob reaches down and pulls a flintlock pistol out of his belt, holding it up to make its presence known—"...when I can bring you in for a small fortune?"

A silent tension creeps into the air, making it difficult to breathe. A few bystanders that have taken notice of the escalating interaction start to get up out of their seats, making their way slowly towards the table. After a few seconds, they have the four of them surrounded. Fiona and Jacob do not react to the growing audience in any way, however. Eira realises the spectators may not in fact be bystanders; it is likely they are subordinates of Fiona and Jacob's, reacting to their commanding officer drawing a firearm.

Eira feels her body tense up as the surrounding mass of bar patrons closes off all their exits. This conflict may have not been about her, but she is nonetheless caught in the middle of it. She tries to take a full breath in, but the capacity of her lungs has been reduced by half, forcing her to take quick, short inhales. As her heartbeat starts to accelerate, a bead of nervous sweat creeps down the side of her head, rolling around the beauty mark on her right cheek.

She jolts slightly as she feels a grip on her hand. She looks down to see the Archman's hand holding hers beneath the table, a gesture which feels somehow like both a reassuring touch and a demand for her to remain calm.

Eira shifts her gaze up to the Archman. His disposition has not changed at all since the conversation began. He maintains his usual composed, stoic spirit as he speaks to Jacob.

"I can pay you your weight in gold for every day you lend me your protection."

Jacob pauses, keeping a finger on the trigger of his pistol as he analyses every one of the Archman's words.

"It's not just the money, *tu sais.* You know, bringing you in would certainly curry favour with the Royal Navy, and

I wouldn't mind getting on their good side. You can't put a *prix* on something as valuable as that. That's priceless."

The Archman blinks a single time, keeping his eyes locked on Jacob's. He surveys Jacob's condition carefully, then crosses his arms and leans back, deciding to change tack.

"Nausea, lack of appetite, redness in the face, constipation, a high fever, and pain in the lower right abdomen. Am I wrong?" the Archman diagnoses.

Jacob looks back at the Archman with a confused hesitancy. "*Pardon?*"

"The symptoms that are plaguing you at this moment. Am I wrong?"

"What does that have to do with anything?!" Jacob says dismissively.

"You have appendicitis."

"The hell are you talking about?!" Jacob frowns, an uneasiness growing in his chest. The sensation pairs nicely with the aching pain in his lower right abdomen.

"It's a malady in your appendix, a part of your lower intestine. If left untreated, it will rupture, giving you an extremely uncomfortable decline into death." Every syllable that comes out of the Archman's mouth is refined by an unfazed confidence.

"*Bien donc.* Well then, if that's the case, then I'd like to die a rich man." Jacob points the barrel of the pistol across the table at the Archman, who still does not move an inch.

"How are you going to spend your earnings in the grave? Wouldn't you rather live a long, prosperous life?"

The barrel of Jacob's pistol lowers as he tries to decipher the Archman's words. "But you just said..."

"I can easily treat the ailment. You'll be better in a week's time."

"*Les hommes* are often willing to say anything when they find themselves at the end of a pistol. Why should I believe you?" Jacob snaps back.

"I am the Archman. Mortal diseases are one of my specialties."

Jacob's frown deepens even further, a stark contrast to the Archman's passive expression. Though he wants to contradict the Archman at every possible opportunity, part of him knows he is being told the undisputed truth.

"He helped me recover from a musket ball wound," Eira interjects, drawing everyone's attention towards her. Jacob and Fiona are intrigued by her claim but are visibly sceptical.

"Let's see." Jacob gestures towards Eira with his pistol.

Eira stands up slowly, careful to not make any sudden movements. She lifts the hem of her shirt up just enough to expose the partially healed wound on the lower right side of her stomach.

Jacob and Fiona are impressed by what they see, though Jacob does everything in his power not to show it.

"You can cure whatever I have?" Jacob turns his attention and his pistol back to the Archman.

"In exchange for your protection," the Archman stipulates.

"And I'll get my weight in gold every day?" Jacob pries.

"Of course."

"*Et tu*, Fiona? You trust him?" Jacob shifts his gaze to Fiona.

"With a face like that, it's *difficile* not to." Fiona gestures subtly towards the Archman.

Jacob pauses for several seconds, deeply contemplating the Archman's proposition. Eira, Fiona, and the Archman wait in silence.

"*Grand-père* Leo said you were a noble man. Let's see if your reputation holds up, *Archomme*."

"So we have an agreement?" The Archman reaches across the table, offering a handshake.

Jacob holsters his pistol back into his belt, then extends his free hand across the table to meet the Archman's.

"*Bien sûr.*"

CHAPTER Seven

A LUXURIOUS ACCUMULATION

"Try to stay well rested." The Archman stands up from the table, Eira following beside him. "Also, no solid food or alcohol for the next twenty-four hours."

"*Quoi?!*" Jacob balls his fists on the table. He would be standing up to confront the Archman at eye level, if it was not completely exhausting to do so.

"You want a safe procedure? No food, no alcohol," the Archman reiterates, turning to head towards the door.

"Where are you going?!" Jacob calls out to him, lifting himself out of his chair slightly, with tremendous effort.

"To prepare for tomorrow. I'll be back shortly."

"*Attendez*! Wait!" Jacob bellows, drawing Eira and the Archman's attention back to him. "Don't take this the wrong way, *mais* I have little trust in you, *Archomme*. I won't have you just slipping away from us."

"I can keep an *oeil* on him," Fiona suggests, moving slowly into the Archman's personal space.

Jacob pauses, looking back and forth between Fiona and the Archman. "Mmm...Okay, *d'accord*." He sits back down abruptly.

"Great!" Fiona joins the Archman and Eira as they leave the inn. "*Allons-y!*"

THE ARCHMAN, EIRA, AND FIONA SIT IN THE DINGHY AS IT makes its way through the bay, towards the Archman's ship.

"*Magnifique...*" Fiona looks up at the massive vessel as they approach the stern, craning her neck upwards to get a better look.

"Where is your crew?" Fiona turns to the Archman, who is occupied with rowing.

"You're looking at it," the Archman replies in a neutral tone.

The dinghy comes to a stop below the upper decks of the ship. The Archman secures the three dangling ropes to the three rings on the dinghy, then pulls the small watercraft up to the platform jutting out.

He locks the pulley mechanism above them and steps out first. He turns back to the dinghy and holds out a hand to help Eira out of the small boat. She takes his hand and steps out carefully this time, making sure to watch the gap between the platform and the dinghy.

"Can I get a hand?"

Eira and the Archman turn back to Fiona, who is standing in the dinghy, reaching out a hand to the Archman.

"You're a Raeburn. You don't need it," the Archman says bluntly.

"*Merde.* My reputation betrays me." Fiona huffs with an exaggerated irritation. She hops out of the dinghy with alacrity, landing gracefully on the platform.

THE ARCHMAN WALKS THROUGH THE DIM CORRIDORS with Eira and Fiona in tow. Fiona marvels at her surroundings the whole way along.

"Did you build all of this *toi-même?*" Fiona asks in astonishment, running a hand across the glossy woodwork.

"Yes, I did it myself. For the most part," the Archman replies.

Eira is finding it difficult to keep up with what Fiona is saying. Her odd accent is manageable enough, but the interspersed French in her syntax makes it quite challenging to fully comprehend her. It does not help that the Archman appears to completely understand everything she says.

They walk down a staircase to the lowest level of decks, then stop outside the combined laboratory–slaughterhouse.

"Do me a favour." The Archman turns to Fiona, holding out the bundle of chains to her. "Keep an eye on her for a while." He indicates towards Eira with a nod of his head.

"*Certainement.*" Fiona takes the bundle of chains in both hands with a smile.

The Archman disappears into the blood-scented room and closes the door behind him, leaving Eira and Fiona alone in the dim corridor.

Fiona looks at the bundle of chains in her hands, following the strands of metal to the collar around Eira's neck. She examines it for a second, trying to make sense of it.

"*Alors*...are you the Archman's *servante*?"

"I...I suppose so. It's complicated," Eira answers tentatively.

"Or are you more like his *chiot*?" Fiona asks.

"His what?"

"A puppy. Are you some kind of pet?"

Eira pauses, caught without a response. She had not really thought about her relationship with the Archman before, much less how it could be defined. From an outsider's perspective, it must look quite unusual. She can only answer by describing the events that led to them being together.

"He attacked the ship I was on a few weeks ago and took me captive. He was planning on eating me."

"*Mon Dieu*..." Fiona is aghast. "*Donc*...So you're his dinner?"

"Well...I hope not," Eira says with a terse exhale. "Fortunately, my fiancé is chasing after us, so I'm much more valuable alive."

"Oh, you have a *fiancé*? Who's the lucky *monsieur?*" Fiona perks up with a giddy energy. It is odd for her to focus on that specific detail out of everything Eira has recounted.

"Roy Kinsley. He's a commodore in the Royal Navy."

Fiona whistles in approval. "*Bien fait*! That's quite the catch! Not exactly my flavour, but I admire the achievement."

"If I don't get eaten, perhaps you can come to the wedding." Eira chuckles pensively.

"Really? *Merci*! *J'adore* weddings!" Fiona smiles jovially. "And good luck not getting eaten."

"Thanks..." Eira nods, chortling slightly.

"Though, I have to say..."—Fiona looks at the door the Archman disappeared behind, her jubilant smile morphing into a significantly more salacious one—"I wouldn't mind getting eaten by *quelqu'un* like him."

"Well, the line starts here," Eira responds, speaking before she has the chance to consider her words.

A moment of stillness lingers in the space between Eira and Fiona. Both of them are equally surprised by Eira's response.

The silence is broken by the Archman opening the door to the laboratory–slaughterhouse; he closes the door behind him as he exits. He looks at Eira and Fiona, both of whom are waiting for him to fill the empty airspace.

"Looks like I'll need some supplies."

"The Econridge market might have what you need." Fiona jumps into the conversation.

"Let's hope so." The Archman takes the bundle of chains back from Fiona, then starts making his way further down the corridor.

Eira and Fiona follow him through the hallway, turning at a corner, where they are met with a much longer hallway. They are both seized by an inquisitive curiosity, as it is their first time in this part of the ship. Unlike the other corridors, there are almost no doorways jutting off on either side until the very end of the hallway, where a single door resides to their right.

The Archman opens the door and enters the space. It is shrouded in complete darkness, but he moves about completely unobstructed.

Eira and Fiona take a few paces into the room, feeling the ground beneath their feet becoming obtrusive and uneven. They look down, trying to identify what is beneath them. It feels like several small pieces of metal, or perhaps rock. The

Archman turns a dial on one of the wall-affixed lamps, igniting it to its maximum output so that its warm light spreads across the room.

Eira and Fiona freeze in place, both consumed by a confounding astonishment. The room is almost ten times the size of all the others, taking up at least a quarter of the ship's capacity. Nearly every inch of the room is filled with all manner of precious metals and jewels. Gold coins pour out across all horizontal surfaces, covering everything in a layer of scintillating luxury. The room is practically overflowing with priceless materials, enough to feasibly buy a small nation.

"*Sacrebleu*..." Fiona looks about, completely baffled. She was not aware it was possible to gather so much wealth in a single spot.

"I was wondering how you were going to pay us so much." Fiona steps further into the room, taking a deeper interest in its contents.

"Is this all yours...?" Eira turns to the Archman, who has grabbed a cloth bag and begun to fill it with fistfuls of gold coins.

"Well, anyone who it might've belonged to has long since died. So for practical purposes, yes." The Archman kneels down to gather some coins from around his feet. Fiona pokes around in the more shadowed regions of the room, moving with the same glint in her eye that crows are known for.

"Where did you find all this?" Eira stays put, still not fully comprehending the sheer amount of material value in her surroundings.

"When I was younger, I gathered it from all my conquests. I fell out of the habit a few centuries ago, however." The Archman walks back to the doorway, where Eira is waiting.

"Let's go." The Archman turns to Fiona, slinging the cloth bag over his shoulder.

"I could spend all day *ici*." With a subtle skip in her step, Fiona adjusts the cap on her head as she rejoins the Archman and Eira. She goes to leave, but the Archman reaches an arm across the doorway, blocking her exit.

"Clearly." He sets down the cloth bag as he narrows his eyes on Fiona, who shifts with an unwieldy energy. Eira takes a step back, sensing the growing tension between the Archman and Fiona.

"Put it all back. Now." The Archman steps close to Fiona, looking down at her with a crippling stare.

"*Quoi?* What are you—" Fiona averts her gaze, laughing nervously under the Archman's crimson glare.

The Archman drops the bundle of chains so both his hands are free. He grabs the cap off Fiona's head. A small collection of gold coins pours off the top of her head onto the ground.

"Got me..." Fiona smiles with an inauthentic innocence as the coins clatter onto the floor. "Anyway, let's get going—"

The Archman suddenly grabs her by her shoulder and wrist, forcing her up against the wall.

"Ah! *Merde!*" Fiona's words are muffled by her face being pressed up against the wall.

The Archman reaches into her pockets and starts pulling out gold coins, silver trinkets, and other pieces of small jewellery. Eira stays at a safe distance, watching the whole process unfold before her with bated breath. Given how capable the Archman is of violence, she is surprised to see him exercising as much restraint as he is. She looks at Fiona, who is quite helplessly pressed against the wooden wall. Despite being completely incapacitated, Eira can still see a faint smile across Fiona's mouth, which surprises her even more than the Archman's physical moderation.

"Anything else?" The Archman speaks tersely to Fiona as he empties out the remains of her pockets. His mouth hovers just a few inches from her ear.

"Er...*oui*. A few necklaces..." Fiona responds.

"Where?"

"Around my neck. Where else?" Fiona raises a coy eyebrow.

The Archman exhales with an irritated timbre. He pulls Fiona away from the wall, keeping one of her arms locked behind her. With his free hand, he reaches into the collar of Fiona's shirt, searching blindly for any remaining pieces of luxury.

"*Oh là-là*, that's no way to treat a lady," Fiona teases. She is clearly not at all bothered by the Archman's physical coercion.

"Sorry, I forgot you were a woman." The Archman rebukes with an unsympathetic detachment, continuing to dig through Fiona's shirt.

"*Vraiment?* Really?" Fiona asks rhetorically. She shifts her upper body slightly, pushing her breast into the Archman's palm. "How about now?"

Eira stays silent as she observes their interaction. She is not sure exactly what she is looking at, but it feels like she is being impolite by watching them engage in such a manner. Nevertheless, she cannot bring herself to look away. She has never seen anyone act in such a blatantly suggestive way. In an effort to try and comprehend it better, she pictures herself in Fiona's position, being accosted by the Archman. After a few seconds of visualising, she decides not to continue, as it is making her face heat up in a most anomalous way.

The Archman does not appear to react at all to Fiona's gesture. He pulls five necklaces out of her shirt and lifts them over her head, pulling her blonde hair up slightly before letting it cascade back over her shoulders.

"You couldn't wait just a little while longer until I started paying you?" he mutters begrudgingly, tossing the necklaces over his shoulder into the unorganised collection of riches behind him.

"*Pardon*, I'm notoriously impatient," Fiona says with a wink.

"That's your problem." The Archman releases his grip on her and picks the bundle of chains back up from the ground. Fiona retrieves her hat from the ground and returns it to her head.

The three of them leave without another word. Eira looks at Fiona and the Archman, startled by how quickly they have moved on from the exchange. Eira is still ruminating over the interaction in her mind. She always thought she had relatively good mental flexibility, but she just cannot wrap her head around what she had just witnessed.

CHAPTER Eight

AN AMICABLE OUTING

Eira and Fiona walk on either side of the Archman as they make their way through the lively streets of Econridge. The Archman is carrying the cloth sack of gold over his shoulder with one hand. In his other, he holds the bundle of chains, the slack of which hangs between him and Eira.

"*Donc*, what do we need?" Fiona looks about as they walk into a market district. The sides of the streets are lined with all sorts of vendors selling all kinds of products: everything from dried foods to construction supplies.

"First, we need to shed some excess weight." The Archman cradles the bundle of chains on his arm so he can reach into the compartment on his belt.

"How so?" Fiona enquires.

The Archman takes a small vial full of white powder out of the compartment and sets down the bundle of chains and bag of coins to free up his hands. He screws off the cap of the vial and pours the contents into the palm of his gloved hand.

"Does this seem like enough?" The Archman reaches his hand out towards Fiona, presenting the small collection of white powder to her.

"Enough of what? *C'est quoi ça*?" Fiona leans forwards, inspecting the white powder curiously.

With a quick exhale, the Archman blows the white powder into Fiona's face. She lurches back for a moment, caught completely off guard. Her surprised expression starts to quickly fade as her eyelids lower and she slouches over.

"*Bâtard...*" Fiona's speech slurs into incomprehensibility as she falls unconscious, right into the Archman's arms.

"What...what was that?" Eira looks back and forth between Fiona and the Archman, struggling to keep up with what is going on.

"Don't worry. She'll wake up in a few hours."

"Okay, but...why?" Eira is not any less perplexed.

"I'm not fond of being chaperoned," the Archman explains.

"Where are you going to put her?" Eira looks around at their busy surroundings. There are not really any optimal spots for storing unconscious individuals.

The Archman surveys their environment, making the same observation as Eira. He spots a vendor a couple of feet away and sees a possible solution. He hoists Fiona's limp body over his shoulder, gathers up the bundle of chains and hands them to Eira, and then picks up the bag of coins. He walks over to the vendor with Eira following at his side.

"Excuse me." The Archman grabs the attention of the vendor with little effort, largely because of his sizeable frame and the fact that he is carrying a comatose person over his shoulder.

"Our friend is taking a bit of a nap. Would you keep an eye on her until she wakes up?" The Archman indicates to Fiona with his head, since both of his hands are full.

"I...uh..." The vendor looks at the eclectic individuals before him, not fully registering the Archman's request.

"That'll be for your trouble." The Archman digs a hand into the cloth bag, pulls out a handful of coins, and presents them to the vendor.

The vendor's eyes light up, his expression suddenly becoming much more welcoming and affable now that there is some kind of currency present.

"Oh, of course. No problem." He receives the random handful of coins from the Archman with a marketable smile.

"Much appreciated." The Archman sets Fiona down so she is sitting with her back against the vendor's stand. He pulls her hat over her eyes slightly so she appears to be sleeping more naturally. It was not entirely necessary, however, as Eira's first encounter with Fiona had made it clear that she could make any kind of physical configuration look like a natural sleeping position.

"Alright then." The Archman takes the bundle of chains back from Eira and they make their way through the marketplace.

Eventually, they come across a stand where medicinal products and cheap alternatives are being sold. After a lengthy cross-examination with the vendor over the legitimacy of certain items, the Archman purchases a few raw herbs and places them in the bag with the coins.

As the Archman finalises the transaction, Eira looks over at the stand beside them. It is laden with all kinds of bread products: rolls, loaves, and many other glutenous nourishments. Her mouth starts to salivate as she realises that she has not eaten anything other than fish for weeks on end. She had recently gotten acclimated to the simplistic seafood diet, but now that the opportunity to diversify her menu has become available, she is starting to crave anything that is not extracted from the ocean.

"Hungry?" the Archman says, making it sound more like an observation than a question.

"No." Eira snaps her attention up to the Archman, reacting in an impulsively defiant manner. She regrets speaking the words the moment they leave her mouth, which is still salivating uncontrollably.

The Archman stares at her a with a patient smirk, waiting for her to respond honestly.

"Yes..." she admits, looking back at the collection of bread on the next stand over, using it as an excuse to avert her gaze.

"I'll go get the fishing rod." The Archman turns away to leave, a smug playfulness in his voice.

Before she can think twice, Eira grabs the chain connecting her to the Archman and yanks on it abruptly. The chain is pulled taut instantly, drawing his attention but not budging him even an inch. It feels like she is trying to uproot a massive tree.

"Something the matter?" the Archman teases.

"Please don't make me ask twice," Eira retorts. She is trying to engage with him using the same level of self-satisfaction, but her growing hunger dulls her edge.

"I won't, but you haven't even asked once." The Archman returns to Eira, releasing the tension in the chain, but maintaining the rhetorical tension between the two of them.

"Fine! Can we buy some goddamn bread?!" Eira bristles, abandoning any shred of tactfulness.

"I don't know..." the Archman says, walking over to the vendor who is tending to the bread stand. He raises a hand to his chin, surveying the wide array of crusted comestibles. "Do you sell any bread that has been damned by God?" he asks the vendor.

Eira shoots the Archman an empty look, the vacancy of expression clearly indicating her irritation with his theatrics.

"For something like that, I'd recommend the pumpernickel." The vendor points to a batch of dark loaves on the lower right side of the stand.

"No thanks." Eira huffs.

"Alright, what can I get you, then?" the vendor asks.

Eira looks up to the Archman, then back to the vendor, concocting a plan for retribution against the Archman's barbaric teasing.

"What's your most expensive product?"

"That'd be the brioche, made with figs, hazelnuts, and blue chee—"

"Great, we'll take all of it."

"Oh...okay!" the vendor says with pleasant surprise as he gathers up the two dozen rolls of soft, auburn-coloured bread.

Eira shoots an obstinate glance up at the Archman, who receives it with a coquettish smile. She would normally have felt bad about the reckless spending of money that did not belong to her, but this occasion is an exception, given the sheer volume of wealth the Archman possesses. It is a drop of water taken from an ocean, making it well worth the retaliation.

The Archman digs through the bag and pulls out a couple of gold coins, counting them in his palm using his thumb. He hands them over to the vendor in exchange for the two dozen rolls which he places into the bag, save for one, which he tosses to Eira.

She bites into the soft piece of brioche, savouring every delectable moment the small roll of bread has to offer. It feels like she is reawakening a dormant sixth sense.

"You get quite insistent when you're famished," the Archman observes candidly, walking away from the bread stand.

Eira goes to speak but hesitates for a moment, as years of conditioning in her youth have programmed out the ability to speak with food in her mouth. She quickly overcomes the hurdle though, as her desire to counter the Archman's comment is much stronger than her desire for etiquette.

"If my hunger offends you, then perhaps you should feed me better."

"Hmm." The Archman smiles in his usual minimalistic way, but then he starts to genuinely consider her suggestion. "We'll be at sea for a while. Perhaps we should gather some provisions."

Eira's eyes light up at his proposition. She fantasises about not needing to go back to eating fish at every meal. It is a deeply appealing reverie.

"Really?" She tries to contain her glee as best she can, but it proves to be a challenging task.

"Unless you'd rather continue eating fish?" the Archman suggests humorously.

"I've eaten enough fish for one lifetime, thank you very much."

"Alright then, anything catch your eye?" The Archman gestures to the entirety of the marketplace.

Eira looks around at the dozens of stalls and stands in their midst, then turns back to the Archman.

"We're going to need some more bags."

THE EVENING SUN STARTS TO SLOWLY CREEP BEHIND THE horizon, causing the sky to gradually slip into a faint darkness. The busy marketplace has decreased significantly in its activity, though there are still a couple of customers milling about.

Among them are Eira and the Archman, whose arms are filled with several large cloth bags, each of which is nearly overflowing with all kinds of foodstuff: dried fruits and meats, baked goods, wheels of cheese, and a couple of bottles of wine.

Most of the bags are hanging off the Archman's large frame, dangling from his back and shoulders and occupying both arms. The weight does not appear to bother him, but the frivolousness of certain purchases certainly does, most notable of which are the dozens of tea bags which Eira is now loading into one of the two bags she is carrying.

"Does this really qualify as a necessity?" the Archman scoffs.

"Of course. If anyone goes a month without tea, they will quickly go insane," Eira quips jovially, continuing to fill the bag.

"I've managed just fine without it."

"Most of us can't survive exclusively on human blood," Eira ripostes.

Eira and the Archman both get a puzzled look from the vendor standing before them.

"...metaphorically speaking, that is." Eira quickly covers their tracks with a light smile, the Archman nodding in accord to lend it legitimacy.

They quickly make their way away from the vendor, as Eira pulls the last couple of coins from the pocket of her pants.

"Seems we've only got enough left for one more inane purchase," the Archman observes sarcastically. "What will it be?"

Eira looks around the marketplace, which has been growing significantly quieter by the minute. Many of the vendors have closed up their stands, and those that have not are in the process of doing so. Something catches Eira's attention on the other side of the street, prompting her to walk over towards it with the Archman in tow.

They arrive before a beggar—an elderly man—who is lying against the stone wall of a building. His bare hands and feet are caked with dirt, which spreads inwards onto his tattered clothing in a diffuse pattern. His right eye is completely gone, either lost due to an unfortunate medical condition, or gouged out in a much more unfortunate circumstance. He has a metal cup in his hand, the bottom of which is filled with a few stray coins.

The beggar does not notice Eira's presence until she has walked right up to him and dropped the remainder of her coins in his cup. The clinking metal sound causes the beggar's head to perk up as he squints his eye to try to get a better look at his donor.

The man looks into his metal cup, then back at Eira, and nods with a warm smile. He clearly wants to thank her for her charity, but it seems as if he is missing his tongue as well. Eira nods in return, then makes her way back to the Archman.

"Are we acquiring some kind of serf?" the Archman asks with a raised eyebrow.

"Of course not. He just needs it more than us," Eira explains.

"What good will it do in his hands? He's got hardly any years left." The Archman looks over at the beggar, genuinely perplexed by Eira's actions.

"He'll have much fewer with an attitude like that."

The Archman pauses, grappling with her logic. The empathetic nature of her gesture makes sense in theory, but witnessing it being applied in real life completely confuses him. There is a look of confounding amazement on his face, one of the many expressions that he has never bothered to fully acquaint himself with.

"*ET VOILÀ!!!*" A booming voice splits the silence of the marketplace, snaring both Eira and the Archman's attention. They immediately know who it is.

"Has it been that long?" the Archman says nonchalantly as he turns around.

Fiona walks up to them, vitriol and vexation leaking out of her very being.

"That was a clever trick, *Archomme. Bien fait.*" Fiona compliments him with seething outrage, crossing her arms and furrowing her brow as much as her face will physically let her.

"Thank you. How was your nap?" the Archman asks plainly.

"Amazing, but that's not *important*." Fiona raises a hand to shush the Archman. "I don't appreciate the conniving tactics."

"I could've knocked you out if you'd rather that."

"I'd rather not be unconscious at all, *merci beaucoup*!" Fiona fumes. "I was willing to be lax before, but after that little stunt, *pas plus.*"

"I wasn't aware you were being lax before," the Archman comments amusingly.

Eira tries to hold back a chortle, but with both hands occupied, it manages to slip past her lips. She had the exact same thought, but unlike the Archman, she was not about to admit it.

"*Très drôle.* Now, let's go." Unamused, Fiona points back in the direction she came from with a curt gesture.

"Go where?" Eira enquires, the smile from the Archman's previous remark still lingering on her face.

"You're spending the night *chez nous*, where I can keep a closer *oeil* on you." Fiona turns her back on Eira and the Archman, but keeps her head turned towards them so she can continue to glare at them.

"You arrived at the perfect time, actually," the Archman says politely.

"*Quoi?*" Fiona turns her body back towards the Archman, her infuriated state mellowing slightly.

"Here." The Archman hands one of the loaded cloth bags to Fiona to lighten his load slightly. She is confused by the offering and looks inside at the collection of food within.

"Thanks," the Archman says with a snide smirk as he starts walking away in the direction of the inn.

"*Fils de pute...*" Fiona curses upon realising that she is being saddled with an unrequested chore instead of being given a gift.

Eira is not sure exactly what Fiona had said, but the tone of her voice made it evident that it was some form of profanity.

"*Je jure*...I'm going to shoot him right in his pretty face," Fiona grumbles as she and Eira rejoin the Archman and walk through the now empty marketplace.

"Again, the line starts here." Eira motions to the space behind her with her head.

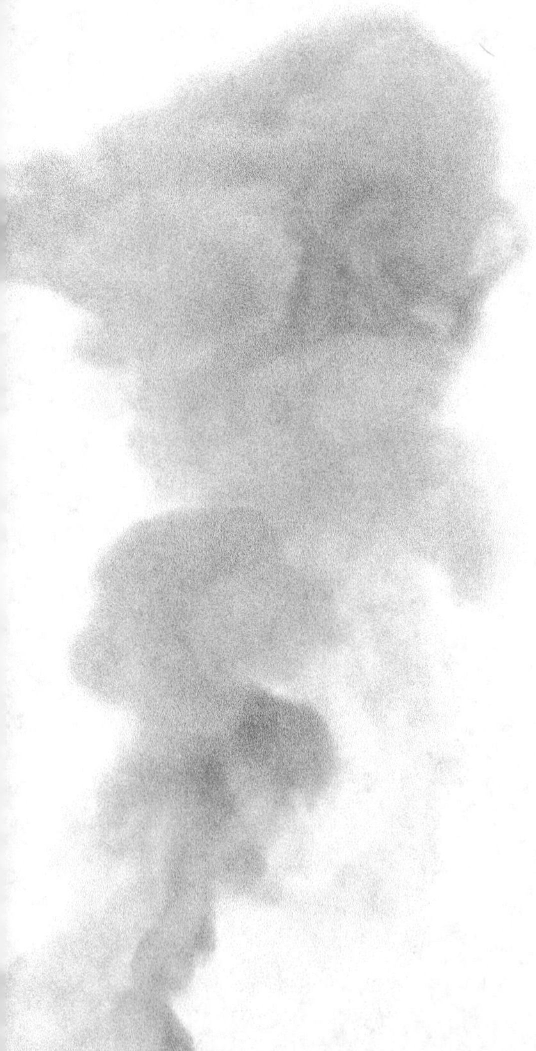

CHAPTER Nine

A PLEASANT RESPITE

"May I—" The Archman starts speaking, but he is quickly interrupted by Fiona shoving him through the open doorway into the inn.

"*Oui, mon Dieu...*" she groans. "Do you really have to ask every single time?"

"It's in my nature," the Archman replies calmly.

Eira follows them into the inn. Fiona, who is still quite agitated, slams the door shut behind Eira with unnecessary force.

The tavern-like lobby of the inn is much emptier than it was several hours ago. Most of the patrons have either departed, retired to their rooms, or been kicked out. One of the tables in the centre of the room is still occupied by Jacob and a few others, who are likely his employees or underlings. They are keeping themselves occupied with drinks and playing cards, except for Jacob, whose lack of participation in the communal intoxication has left him quite irritable. He has a stern frown on his face which almost perfectly matches Fiona's. Due to his unimpaired vision, he is the first to notice Fiona walk in with Eira and the Archman.

"Back *encore?*" he comments laconically as they walk over to him. He looks at the large amount of bags being carried between the three of them, taking a superficial interest in them.

"This must be quite a complicated procedure if you need *tout ça,*" he jokes, reaching his arms up to stretch them.

"This isn't all for you. But yes, it's not exactly simple," the Archman explains.

"*Je sais, je sais.* I know it," Jacob says. "So what are you doing back here?" Jacob lowers his arms, crossing them across his chest in typical Raeburn fashion.

"*L'Archomme* pulled a little stunt and drugged me. It goes *sans dire*, he's staying here for tonight."

"*Eh?*" Jacob exclaims with a confused reservation. He does not want to react too overtly, in case Fiona is telling a humorous fib. Jacob is aware— more than anyone— of her penchant for doing so.

"I don't take kindly to supervision," the Archman responds with an off-handed passiveness.

"He didn't do anything to you, did he?!" Jacob speaks with a sudden increase of intensity. He would be on his feet if it did not require obscene amounts of energy to lift himself out of his chair.

"I wish, but *non.* Just left me with some vendor and went off." Fiona crosses her arms as she gripes.

"You live up to your reputation, *Archomme.*" Jacob turns his gaze to the Archman with a harsh indignation.

“Likewise,” the Archman retorts.

“I’ll have one of the *gouvernantes* prepare their rooms,” Fiona says to Jacob as she walks towards the staircase. The Archman and Eira follow close behind.

“We’ll take just one room, thanks,” the Archman interjects.

Fiona walks up the first step of the staircase but quickly halts and turns back towards Eira and the Archman. There is an interrogative curiosity about her.

“Forgive my asking...is she your *mademoiselle*?” She looks at the Archman, pointing to Eira with her thumb.

Eira halts in place, looking back and forth between Fiona and the Archman. They are both standing a foot higher than her: Fiona because of her place on the staircase, and the Archman from his naturally large stature. It is not a particularly pressing question that Fiona posed, and yet Eira desperately wants to know how the Archman will respond.

“She’s my collateral. She stays with me, no matter what,” the Archman answers with such certainty that it leaves no room for compromise.

It had been the answer Eira was expecting, and yet something in the way the Archman said it resonates with her in a way that is inexplicably satisfying. She can almost feel the effect of his words as a physical sensation, like a light tingling in her stomach which spreads across her lower abdomen. Upon closer inspection, though, it might have just been her wound acting up momentarily.

“*Bien,* that makes it easier for us.” Fiona shrugs indifferently. The tone of her words contrasts with the look in her eyes, which suggests a genuine investment in the Archman’s answer.

“Also, I have a request.” The Archman reclaims Fiona’s attention before she can turn away.

"*Je dois dire,* I'm impressed with how much audacity one person can have," Fiona scoffs.

"She needs a bath." The Archman points to Eira.

Eira is not fond of the fact she is being referred to like she is not present, but it is true that she is in desperate need of a wash.

"*Vraiment?*" Fiona looks at the Archman with an exasperated tiredness.

"Really. Unless you don't mind her dirtying your sheets," the Archman continues.

"Whatever," Fiona says dismissively, making her way up the staircase.

"Is this really necessary?" Eira asks, knowing that her question will not really change the Archman's mind.

She is sitting in a heavy, white bathtub, the warm water coming up to her bare neck, covering her naked body with a vague translucency. It provides a scarce amount of modesty, which would not bother her if she was alone, but that is not the case.

The Archman sits on the ground, leaning against the bathtub. His back faces Eira so they are unable to see one another out of their peripheral vision.

"Given your inability to stay put when told to do so, I think this is very much necessary."

"You make me sound like a problematic pet." Eira smiles faintly as she takes a bar of soap from a dish next to the tub.

"If you didn't act like one, then I wouldn't describe you as such." The Archman returns the light smile, neither of them aware they made the exchange.

"Well, at least I don't bite." Eira holds her damp black hair in her hands, running the bar of soap across the strands to cover it with suds.

"I don't particularly mind biting," the Archman admits.

"What?" Eira pauses with a twinge of confusion.

"It would be awfully hypocritical if I did."

Eira turns her head to look behind her, not quite following the Archman's logic.

He turns his head to face her, so they are just barely able to see one another. He grins with the right side of his face, exposing one of the glistening white fangs in his mouth.

Eira suddenly realises what he is referring to. She quickly turns back around and goes back to lathering her hair. The Archman pulls his gaze away at a much slower pace, his eyes lingering briefly on her neck. The light dampness of the water gives it quite a tantalising look.

"Do...do you ever actually use them?" Eira asks hesitantly. She is not sure if it is an offensive or insensitive question, since she has never known anyone with a pair of carnivorous appendages before.

"It's been a while since I have. It's a relic from a more prehistoric part of my life. Sort of like your tailbone."

"My what?"

"The bone at the base of your spine. It serves no purpose; it's just the remains of when you used to be primates."

There are a lot of things being said which Eira is having trouble grasping. For a moment she is uncertain whether he is being facetious, but in the time she has known him, he almost never engages in lighthearted deceitfulness.

"What do you mean by 'primates'?" Eira asks, trying not to sound as lost as she evidently was.

"Your human ancestors were primitive creatures. They had tails," the Archman elucidates. "The tailbone is left over from that period of your existence."

"You mean...we used to be animals?"

"Millions of years ago, yes." The Archman nods, a sly smile slowly creeping across his lips. "To be honest, I don't know if you've changed all that much."

Eira does not respond. She is heavily preoccupied, trying to reassemble her entire worldview after the Archman just casually shattered it into a thousand pieces. She quickly gives up, though, deciding that it would be a task that would need to be done over a long period of time.

"How's the wound?" the Archman asks, changing the subject much more nonchalantly than seems appropriate to Eira.

"Since you last asked me? No different." Eira chortles.

"It could've gotten worse in the time since I asked you," the Archman retorts defensively.

"You mean in the last two minutes? I doubt that," Eira says with a clever demeanour. She relishes every opportunity she has to one-up the Archman, who rarely lets his rhetorical guard down.

"Careful, princess," the Archman warns with a playful timbre.

"Are you still calling me that?" Eira lets out an irritated sigh, though she is still smiling.

"Yes, I think it suits your pompous attitude quite well." The Archman chuckles.

"I don't appreciate the baseless derisions, thank you," Eira deflects.

"Baseless? How about all the food you made me buy for you?"

"Food is an essential item. How does that make me pompous?"

"And what about the tea?" the Archman quips.

"Highly essential! We've talked about this!" Eira retorts with a passionate sarcasm, causing some of the bathwater to jostle out of the tub.

Eira walks alongside the Archman, both of them following Fiona through the inn until they arrive at their designated room. Fiona opens the door and Eira walks inside, taking note of the interior.

It is a small but comfortable room with all the necessary furnishings and a few extra amenities, like a narrow bookshelf against one of the walls, and a cushioned chair in the corner beside the bed. The lack of space is further exacerbated by the floor space being occupied by the many cloth bags of food bought earlier in the day. The room is lit warmly with a single candle on the bedside table.

Eira looks at the bed quizzically; it has enough room to generously accommodate a single person, but not quite enough for two people, unless they were to sleep in an intimate embrace. And with the Archman's large frame, they would need to close the gap even more. Eira can feel her heart rate slowly increase as she tries to tackle this issue.

"*Donc,* it's a bit cramped for two people," Fiona says to the Archman as they both look into the room.

"So it seems," the Archman concurs.

"If you're worried about her getting *en dehors*, I could have one of my men guard the door. You wouldn't need to watch her all night."

"Oh?" the Archman enquires with healthy scepticism. "So I could have my own room?"

"*En fait*, we're pretty booked up for the night," Fiona says with a tone that does not inspire complete honesty.

"My bed is big enough for two, though," she suggests suggestively.

"I suppose that'll come in handy in case you put on some weight." The Archman turns away from Fiona and steps into the room with a sardonically courteous nod. He was right to be sceptical.

"*Bonsoir*," he says politely as he shuts the door.

Eira sits on the end of the bed awkwardly, still grappling with the sleeping arrangement conundrum.

Meanwhile, the Archman takes the coiled bundle of chains which he was carrying with him and sets it down on the bedside table. He had removed Eira's collar for her bath, not necessarily for her convenience, but rather to prevent the chain from rusting.

The Archman walks over to the bookshelf and reads the spines of the few books strewn upon the dusty shelves. He picks one out and walks over to the chair in the corner of the room. He removes his black cloak, draping it across the back of the seat, before sitting down and opening the book.

Eira watches him as he does all this, waiting for some kind of cue from him to resolve the bedding issue.

The Archman looks up from his book at her, their eyes meeting for a moment of silence.

"Can I help you?" the Archman asks plainly.

"I...um..." Eira fumbles over her thoughts, resulting in her tripping over her words.

"Do you need a kiss goodnight or something?" he jabs whimsically.

"What?! No! I just..." Eira snaps defensively but catches herself before she plays too far into the Archman's hands. It takes a moment for her pulse to calm down and for the redness to leave her face. "Where are you going to sleep?"

"Don't worry about it," the Archman replies simply.

"Why not?" Eira pries.

"It doesn't matter."

"If you don't tell me why, I'm only going to get more worried," Eira asserts.

The Archman pauses for half a second, then sits back in his chair to make himself a bit more comfortable.

"I don't need to sleep for another few years. So it doesn't matter."

"What..." Eira only found herself more confused after the Archman's response. It is a feeling that she has become well acquainted with in his presence.

"My sleep cycle isn't exactly like yours," the Archman explains. "It takes a total of ten years: awake for seven, asleep for three."

"Oh," Eira mutters. Now that the Archman has clarified it, it answers many previous questions. She had been wondering why he was willing to give up his bedroom so easily, and why she had never seen him in a sleepy state before.

"You're just full of surprises," Eira says with a smirk as she climbs into the bed and pulls the covers over her.

"Likewise." The Archman reciprocates with a smirk of his own.

Eira turns over in the bed and gets comfortable as the Archman goes back to his book.

After a day on her feet, it is a huge relief to finally be able to rest. She feels like she could fall asleep mere seconds after closing her eyes. Before she does so, she glances over her shoulder at the Archman, who is reading silently by the candlelight.

The bed is not any more or any less comfortable than the Archman's, but something certainly feels different about going to sleep in this situation. Even before being taken captive, she was used to sleeping entirely on her own. She assumed having another person in the room with her as she tried to doze off would make it more challenging, but it was nearly the exact opposite. Having the Archman watching over as she drifted to sleep gave her a strange feeling of serenity and security.

CHAPTER
Ten

A REPUDIATED REQUEST

Dozens of lit candles ignite the large bathroom, scattered in an organised manner about the room to maximise the illumination since the windows are closed. Jacob sits on a wooden table in the centre of the room; Eira, Fiona, and the Archman stand around him.

"The mood lighting feels a bit *macabre*," Jacob comments as he undoes the buttons on his white shirt. "Can't we just open a *fenêtre?*"

"Afraid not," the Archman replies as he pulls several surgical instruments out of his cloth sack and sets them on the table in an orderly fashion.

Jacob looks down at the growing collection of sharp implements and utensils, many of which are completely unrecognisable. He is not sure whether he should be relieved or concerned by their lack of familiarity.

"Don't worry, you'll be asleep the whole time," the Archman says, continuing to pull medical implements out of the sack.

"That's precisely *pourquoi* I'm worried," Jacob retorts, pulling his shirt off his shoulders and tossing it aside.

"I'll be keeping an *oeil* on him." Fiona reassures him, shooting a glance at the Archman which could be interpreted as either infatuation or hostility, perhaps both. "If Jacob doesn't walk out of this *chambre*, then neither will you."

"He won't be walking for a little while," the Archman quips, not bothering to look up from his bag.

"You know what I mean," Fiona says tersely.

"How long will it take?" Jacob asks, deciding to remove his boots as well.

"About an hour." The Archman takes the needle and syringe from the table and starts to connect them into a single instrument. He continues to assemble the appliance from muscle memory as he turns to Eira.

"It would go faster with some assistance, however."

"What?" Eira straightens her posture, now that she has suddenly become the centre of attention.

"Since you're so adamant about making yourself useful, I thought you might like to aid me?" The Archman twists the chamber of the syringe into place, secures it to the needle, and sets it down.

"I...I've never done anything like this before. Is that really wise?" Eira pulls at the collar around her neck, a nervous tick which she is beginning to adopt after being leashed for nearly a month.

"You would just be following my instructions," the Archman explains.

"Well..." Eira looks away to take on the appearance of being deep in thought, despite her mind being entirely blank.

"I'll do it." Fiona encroaches, so that she is on the opposite side of the Archman as Eira.

"You will?" the Archman enquires, his interest neither piqued nor dulled.

"It makes more sense. *De plus,* I think Jacob would prefer it that way," Fiona reasons, pointing towards Jacob.

"*Vraiment?* With your clumsy fingers—" Jacob is interrupted by a well-placed kick to his shin from Fiona which goes largely unnoticed beneath the table.

"*Garce...*" Jacob swears as he leans over to rub his shin, but quickly decides against it, since it exacerbates the aching pain in his abdomen.

"Alright, put these on." The Archman takes a pair of leather gloves from his cloth bag and hands them to Fiona, who puts them on eagerly.

"Come on, then." The Archman takes the chain attached to Eira's collar and pulls it with enough force to get her attention.

"Pardon?" Eira turns to him and steps forward to release some of the tension in the chain.

"You don't need to be here. I'm sure it will bore you, regardless." The Archman starts guiding her to the door.

"Oh." Eira should have expected as much, and yet it still catches her off guard. She has spent so much time in the Archman's company, it now feels strange to be separated from him.

The Archman leads Eira out of the bathroom and through the hallways of the inn until they reach the bedroom, the door to which he holds open for her to enter. He turns around and starts locking the chain to the handle of the door, the most easily accessible anchor in his vicinity.

"Won't you be gone for just an hour?" Eira asks.

"I will. What's your point?" The Archman turns the key in the padlock before removing it and returning the key to a compartment on his belt.

"Do you really need to do all this?" Eira points to the door handle, which now has several chain links lashed around it.

"If I don't, will you behave yourself?" The Archman answers her question with a question of his own.

"Am I not usually well-behaved?" Eira answers his question to a question with a question of her own.

"By my observation, you've got quite an inclination toward naughtiness." The Archman smirks with his usual reserved composure. While his mouth does not convey much, his crimson eyes display an evident smugness.

The context in which the Archman spoke was nothing disconcerting, but Eira cannot help but interpret his words to mean something far more salacious. It instantly brings a bright redness to her face, which complements the Archman's smug eyes quite nicely.

"Maybe you should make a closer observation, then." Eira crosses her arms and looks away, trying to cover up her flustered temperament.

"Oh?" The Archman walks across the room to close the distance between them. It only takes a few paces, thanks to his large stride. He looks down at Eira for a few seconds, perusing her in her unsettled state. His eyes pass across her neck for much longer than any other part of her anatomy.

It had not occurred to Eira that the Archman would take her challenge so literally. She feels helpless to repel him in this circumstance. It is in moments like these she wishes she had Fiona's unflinching resolve.

"I think my conclusion was quite accurate." The Archman turns away, nodding his head as he reaffirms his observation.

Eira can feel a weight lift from her shoulders as she is freed from the Archman's oppressive gaze, but the lack of force upon her body leaves her with a strange coldness.

"I believe your theory could use some revisions," Eira jests, trying to get the last word in as the Archman makes his way to the door.

"You're not fooling anyone but yourself, princess." He finishes the repartee with a final quip and closes the door behind him as he exits.

Eira looks around the empty room, looking for something to occupy her for the next hour. She has a lingering thought in the back of her head that she cannot shake: she would not be here if she had simply accepted the Archman's request for assistance. As a result of her indecision, he is now in Fiona's company instead of hers.

KINSLEY AND NORMOND WALK THROUGH A MASSIVE, SPAcious hallway, guided along by a well-dressed guide. The scent of wig powder and marble polish fill the air, the trademark aroma of prestige and bureaucracy. Normond takes in the surroundings with a fascinated appreciation, as it is his first time inside a building of such high esteem.

There are all sorts of couriers and servicemen moving about, many of whom are carrying armfuls of documents back and forth. No matter how large the load they carry, however, they each walk with an upright posture. In this environment, no one would be caught dead with slouched shoulders or a curved spine.

The guide escorts Kinsley and Normond to a pair of large doors, the outsides of which are embellished with an array of gold and silver. Kinsley surveys the two large doors, subconsciously comparing them to the ones that lead into his own office.

The guide takes hold of a brass doorknob and pushes the heavy panel inwards. He steps a few paces inside, then turns around to hold the entryway open for Kinsley and Normond.

Normond goes to take a step through the doorway, but, without a word, Kinsley holds an arm up to halt him. Normond steps back dubiously, looking up to Kinsley with a reluctant confusion. Kinsley raises a single finger, indicating that they need to wait.

"Now presenting Commodore Roy Kinsley and Captain Callum Normond of the Fourth Naval Division," the guide announces.

Kinsley steps through the doorway, followed quickly by Normond. Once they have entered the room, the guide exits promptly, closing the door behind himself.

Kinsley and Normond now find themselves in an elegant office space. Wide transparent windows make up a large portion of the wall space, allowing the room to fill with sunlight. The room has a kind of sophistication that is similar to Kinsley's, but it accomplishes this elevated atmosphere in a much different fashion. The floor and wall space are left mostly unoccupied by furnishing and decorations, letting the room's natural architecture speak for itself.

Of the few pieces of furniture, there is a modestly sized desk located in the corner of the room. Getting up from said desk is a man who is very clearly making the transition from middle to old age: Darion Wilcox. His thinning hair has lost most of its dark colour, and his face is bordered with several creases, like contour lines on a topographical map. His physique, which was once strong and refined by years of naval training, has begun to atrophy from years of desk work.

There is clearly no attempt on his part to mask his ageing. He wears his faded grey hair and creased facial features like badges of honour, right next to the actual badges on the left breast of the suit which is now half a size too large for him. In spite of his age, he moves towards Kinsley and Normond with an expedient directness, a stark contradiction to the frail image that his body puts forth.

"Commodore, Captain. Good afternoon." Wilcox nods politely to Kinsley and Normond as he approaches them.

"Good afternoon, Sir. Thank you for seeing us." Kinsley nods in return.

Normond follows Kinsley's example and nods courteously, though he bends over to such a degree that it seems more like a light bow rather than a nod.

"Come, take a seat." Wilcox gestures back to his desk, where two chairs are waiting in front of it.

The three men make their way to the desk, each of them sitting down at their own pace.

"I read your letter requesting an audience about a week ago." Wilcox adjusts himself in his chair, searching for the position which will put the least amount of strain on his body. "My memory's not what it used to be, so I'll have to ask you to remind me the reason for your being here."

"Certainly." Kinsley reaches into the breast pocket of his jacket and pulls out an envelope from which he extracts a folded piece of paper. "We're just here for a signature."

"A signature for what exactly?" Wilcox takes the paper from Kinsley, sliding it across the desk until it hangs over the edge, so it is easier to pick up.

"It is a request to mobilise the reserved divisions immediately," Kinsley explains.

"Beg your pardon?" Wilcox raises his gaze from the page, up to Kinsley.

"The reserved divisions," Kinsley reiterates with a nod.

"Are we at war, Commodore?" Wilcox sets down the page, leaning back into his chair and meshing his fingers.

"In some ways, yes." Kinsley leans in to keep the distance between himself and Wilcox the same.

"And who are we at war with? And why haven't I been informed?" Wilcox cross-examines with a furrowed brow.

"You're being informed right this moment, Sir." Kinsley points down to the page between himself and Wilcox. "Approximately one month ago, one of our ships was attacked by the Archman. He took three hostages: two of whom we believe to have already perished, and the third currently being held captive."

"The Archman..." Wilcox raises a sceptical eyebrow, his fingers meshing deeper together. He looks back and forth between Kinsley and Normond in silence, trying to assess whether or not he is being used as the butt of some intricate joke.

"Commodore, if I was in search of theatrics, I would go to the theatre. You mean to tell me we were attacked by the Archman?"

“I met him myself, as did Captain Normond here.” Kinsley gestures to Normond, who nods in silent accord. “He is quite real, Sir. I assure you. I have an entire crew that can attest to that as well.”

Wilcox muses for a moment before turning back to Kinsley.

“That’s certainly a jarring discovery...” Wilcox wrings his hands slightly, keeping his fingers meshed all the while. “...but I must admit, this is beyond excessive.”

Kinsley freezes with a troubled perplexion. He quickly recomposes himself, presenting a respectful tone. “Pardon?”

“Would you use a cannon to dispose of a rat? Of course not. I can’t allow the use of the reserved divisions because of a single man, even if he is the Archman. They are reserved for good reason,” Wilcox decrees.

“Sir, I must ask you to reconsider.” Kinsley pushes the page on the desk towards Wilcox.

“If we waged war on every single lowlife that attacked us, we would be at war with half of the Atlantic Ocean. This is simply not the rational course of action.”

“If I might, Sir...” Normond interjects timidly. “...the hostage that was taken was Commodore Kinsley’s fiancée.”

Wilcox receives the additional information with a surprised stillness. He takes a deep breath, then turns to Kinsley with a softer tone.

“You have my sympathy, Commodore, but I’m afraid that’s all I can offer you. I’ve had many officers like yourself come to me asking for radical military action whenever they lose a loved one to piracy. It may seem cruel, but it is just a fact of nature. And that is especially true for someone like the Archman.”

Kinsley sits motionlessly, his fists and jaw locked with an immobile tension. Rigidity spreads throughout his whole body.

He grabs the page from Wilcox's desk and stands up abruptly, leaving without another word.

"Ah, thank you for seeing us, Sir." Normond stands up and does another nod–bow before rushing after Kinsley, who makes his way out of the office, tension in his brow and aggravation in his chest.

CHAPTER Eleven

A THWARTED ADVANCE, PART 1

Eira sits up abruptly in bed, clutching the sheets in her hands with white knuckles. It takes her a few seconds to regulate her accelerated heart rate and sporadic breathing as she slowly loosens her grip on the bedsheets.

"Troubling dreams, princess?" The Archman lifts his gaze from the book in his hands and shifts it over to Eira.

Eira, continuing to reclaim control of her lungs and heart, looks forwards in blank silence.

"Eira?" This time his words reach her; she is not used to hearing him say her name.

She turns towards the Archman, who is sitting in his chair at her bedside, right where he was when she fell asleep.

"Ah...I'm fine," she says, trying to convince herself more than anyone else.

"Hardly seems like it." The Archman sets aside his book and briefly stands up from his chair before taking a seat on the end of the bed. "Do you frequently experience night terrors?"

"No, I don't..." Eira says quietly. "It wasn't a nightmare."

"Hmm. You must have quite the exhilarating imagination." The Archman raises a hand to his chin as he ponders amusingly.

"I'm not sure that's it." Eira pushes her black hair out of her face, her fingers quickly getting tangled in the mess of dark locks.

"I'll get a bath running," the Archman says as he gets up from the bed, taking notice of Eira's jumbled collection of hair.

"Oh, no, I'm fine thanks—"

"I'm sure you are, but it's more for the sake of those in your surroundings." The Archman retrieves his black cloak from the chair and dusts it off.

Eira subtly lifts her arm up to inconspicuously inspect her hygiene. Even if she were to theoretically lack any sense of smell, the large stains of sweat under both her armpits would make it quite clear that she is not at prime cleanliness.

Eira wishes that she would produce a more aromatic perspiration, like the kind of rugged primal scent that the Archman has. Instead, she emits a fragrance which inspires something more akin to livestock.

"I'll be back in a bit." The Archman pulls the hood of his cloak over his head as he exits the room, closing the door behind him.

The Archman turns a key in the lock on Eira's collar, opening up the metal restraining device and freeing her neck. Eira brings her hand up to her nape and tilts her head from side to side to stretch the muscles beneath.

The familiar, heavy, enamel-covered bathtub rests a few feet in front of her. It is filled most of the way with hot water, which releases the occasional wisp of steam.

"The longer you take, the colder it gets," the Archman comments as he coils up the length of chain in his hands.

"Is that so? I wasn't aware," Eira retorts sardonically as she begins undressing. The Archman smirks and turns his back to Eira, continuing to gather up the chain.

Eira has become relatively comfortable being disrobed in the Archman's presence, though she still reserves a certain amount of awkwardness from his company.

This morning, however, she feels an unusual level of embarrassment as she looks down at the bathtub. This bathroom had been the precise location of her dream last night. Her present circumstances feel very similar to her drowsy fantasy, the main exception being that in her nightly vision, she was not the only one getting naked. Eira feels her face flush with colour as she recalls the visuals produced by her slumbering subconscious.

After removing her sweat-stained nightgown, Eira lowers herself into the bathtub. The stinging heat of the water helps to distract her from her own thoughts.

The Archman takes his place sitting on the floor with his back leaning against the tub, coiling up the last of the chain as he sits down.

"How's the water?" he asks as he sets the chain aside.

"Wet," Eira replies.

"Brilliant examination, Doctor Pryce." The Archman chortles.

"I'm surprised you remember my last name," Eira remarks, her tone suggesting a lighthearted insult, but her genuine surprise making it more of a compliment.

"It's common courtesy to remember the names of those close to you," the Archman replies with an exaggerated candour.

"It's also common courtesy to tell someone your name when you meet them," Eira counters.

"For my purposes, it's a bit redundant."

"How so?"

"Do you introduce yourself to your meals before eating them?"

"I guess not." Eira chuckles at the absurd concept. "But if my meal was another person, then it might be the polite thing to do."

"Hmm. Alright, how about this..." The Archman props a knee up to rest his hand on as he concocts a wager. "If you can guess my name correctly, then I'll let you go."

Eira pauses as she considers his proposal. For a moment, she is not sure how badly she actually wants her freedom. Regardless, she knows that she definitely wants to figure out his name.

"And what happens if I lose?"

"Hmm..." The Archman ponders for a few seconds, a wicked grin coming across his mouth. "If you lose, then I get to turn around."

Eira can feel the blood rush right back to her face, undoing the past several minutes of effort to calm herself down. The water suddenly feels very cold, relative to her own body's temperature. Despite her cardiovascular system's intense reaction to the Archman's proposition, she maintains a level head.

"How many guesses do I get?"

"Let's say...thirty."

"You seem quite assured of yourself," Eira quips as she runs a few fingers through her hair.

"I have good reason to be." He nods with a self-assured smile.

"Alright, you're on." Eira smiles.

"Go right ahead, then," the Archman invites with a taunting angle to his words.

"Matthew?"

"No."

"John?"

"Nope."

"Luke?"

"No."

"David?"

"No."

"Noah?"

"Not quite."

"Isaiah?"

"No."

"Peter?"

"Afraid not."

"Paul?"

"No."

"Adam?"

"Just keep reciting biblical names, I'm sure it'll work eventually." The Archman laughs to himself.

"Alright...Bradley?"

"No."

"Clayton?"

"Nope."

"Elliot?"

"No."

"Herman?"

"Do I look like a Herman to you?"

"I don't know!" Eira huffs.

The Archman's appearance does not provide any kind of clue to what his name might be. His puzzling accent, combined with his blood-red eyes and silver hair, makes it impossible to place his ethnicity. Even if she could, his ageless nature would make it all the more challenging to identify his name. She is clearly at a disadvantage, and yet she cannot help but enjoy herself.

"Cecil?"

"No."

"Richar—"

Eira finds herself interrupted by a loud wooden slam coming from somewhere else in the inn. Though the sound was quite heavily muted by several walls and a whole floor, the fact they were able to hear it at all meant that it must have been quite loud at the source.

Eira and the Archman both turn to the door of the bathroom, then look to one another in unison. There is a moment of silence, which is quickly filled by the increasing sound of human activity from inside the inn.

"What was that?" Eira instinctively brings her legs to her chest to cover herself.

The Archman stands up and keeps listening to the growing activity coming from outside of the bathroom. The playful atmosphere has completely evaporated, replaced by a sceptical apprehension.

"I'll go take a look." He goes to the bathroom door and pulls the hood of his black cloak over his head. "Stay here."

The door shuts quickly behind him, leaving Eira alone in the bathtub. Strangely enough, she feels less safe now that the Archman has gone.

THE ARCHMAN DESCENDS THE STAIRCASE TO THE MAIN tavern-like lobby of the inn. Just as the auditory cues had suggested, there is an unseasonably large gathering of people for this time of year. This congregation is segregated into two distinct mobs. The larger of the two stands right in the entryway of the inn, composed of many tough-looking characters, all of whom are carrying some kind of rough-looking weapon. They look like a miscellaneous assortment of bounty hunters, mercenaries, and sell-swords. At the front of this mob is a short, widely built man, who looks to be the roughest of the batch.

Squared off against him is Fiona, the leader of the second mob, which has gathered behind her in response to the larger mob making a most unwelcome entrance. There are many familiar faces in this group: they belong to Fiona and Jacob's large crew of subordinates.

The Archman arrives at the base of the staircase and pulls the hood of his cloak up to disguise himself even more. He blends himself into the bystanders that are not part of either mob. He can sense the tension in the air, and the impending violence brewing beneath it.

"*Malheureusement,* I don't think we have enough rooms for you all," Fiona says with a snarky tone, her arms crossed firmly over her chest.

"That's fine. We won't be staying long." The stocky man's voice matches his appearance quite perfectly. "Unless you plan on holding us up."

"*C'est bien*. How can we help you?" Fiona does not budge an inch.

The stocky man holds up a sheet of paper, which contains a printed illustration of the Archman upon it, with some bold lettering located above and below.

"We have business with one of your patrons who is staying here."

Fiona looks at the sheet of paper and identifies it as one of the many wanted posters which have been circulating.

"*Non*...if we had someone as *beau* as him staying here, I'd be the first to know." She shakes her head.

"Bullshit. We've had plenty of witnesses say that you've been hiding the Archman here." The stocky man pushes the page further into Fiona's field of vision, as if to drive his point home.

Fiona pauses for a second, contemplating the best course of action.

"Even if he was here, I would *jamais* sell out a fellow outlaw."

The stocky man and Fiona lock eyes. The two mobs behind them each grip their weapons tighter.

"It's his head or yours, lady. You decide."

"*Attendez*, you're forgetting a third option." Fiona raises a finger, a vicious glare overtaking her azure eyes. "Your head is also on the table."

There is a split second of calm after Fiona finishes speaking, but it is short-lived, as the stocky man pulls a shortsword from a sheath and thrusts it towards Fiona's abdomen. Having anticipated the attack, Fiona pulls a hidden dagger from the inside of her vest, parries the shortsword, and evades the strike.

Chaos immediately rings out as the two mobs clash with one another. The havoc immediately escalates in brutality, the skirmish growing with barbaric intensity every second. The sound of blades clanging and flintlocks firing is overcut with screams of gore and savagery. Bystanders run for cover, trying to distance themselves from the conflict as much as possible.

"Spread out! Find the Archman!" the stocky man bellows as he exchanges blows back and forth with Fiona. The larger mob starts to fan out across the inn, quickly overtaking the space.

Before the Archman can react and come up with a rational solution, he is drawn into the mayhem as one of the bounty hunters rushes at him with a club. The Archman catches the blunt instrument in his hand and pulls it out of the bounty hunter's hand effortlessly. He looks down at his soon-to-be victim for half a second, before grabbing him by his hair and slamming his head down into the ground with cataclysmic force.

As the Archman drops the bloodied bounty hunter to the floor, it becomes clear that this conflict will not be subduing itself anytime soon. Force will be the most expedient way to end it.

The Archman lowers his head and weaves his way into the fray, picking up an abandoned cutlass from the ground to arm himself with. Whenever danger approaches him, he cuts it down with a single, merciless slash. Amid the hectic cruelty of his surroundings, the Archman keeps himself present and level-headed. In a mass turmoil such as this, it becomes a challenge to separate friend from foe, so the Archman opts to simply strike down those who attack him first.

The difference in size of the two mobs slowly diminishes as the Archman's combat expertise helps to even the odds. Nevertheless, the invading mob is able to easily spread out and conquer the inside of the inn. They break into every room they come across, surveying the establishment for every possible hiding spot, oblivious that their target is right before them.

The Archman notices the marauding mob moving throughout the inn, causing a terrifying thought to snap into his head. He turns his attention to the staircase he had descended from and spots several armed men rushing up it and disappearing onto the upper floors.

"SHIT!!!" The Archman bolts towards the staircase with sudden urgency.

Back in the bathroom, Eira sits with her legs against her chest and her arms wrapped around her shins as she listens to the cacophony of battle noises ringing out from the lobby of the inn. She shivers with a tense agitation—the cold bathwater only exacerbates her anxieties.

Standing out from the savage symphony is a set of footsteps which quickly make their way up to the bathroom door. Eira turns her attention to the closed door and holds her breath as it swings open suddenly.

Eira feels a cold shudder run up the length of her spine as an unfamiliar face barges into the bathroom, with an unfamiliar body beneath. She makes eye contact with the stranger for a moment as they are each taken aback by an initial shock, neither of them expecting to be met with one another's presence. That preliminary surprise which they both share quickly devolves into two greatly different reactions, however.

Eira's body freezes stiff, her muscles contracting in a defensive rigidity, her bare skin lining itself with a coarse pattern of goosebumps. In contrast, the marauding individual takes a leisurely step forwards into the bathroom and closes the door behind himself.

"Sorry to barge in..." The man walks across the spacious bathroom, towards Eira. As he approaches her, he sheathes the shortsword that he was carrying.

The gesture does little to ease Eira's nerves, which are thoroughly shot. She feels paralysed by the man's mere presence, which has a distinctly predacious quality to it.

"Didn't realise someone was in here." The man stops before the bathtub, looking down at Eira in her uncovered state. His glare makes Eira's stomach drop.

Eira opens her mouth to speak, taking several seconds to voice her thoughts, which are racing at three times their normal pace. "Can I help you?"

"I'm sure you can." The foraying man smiles and squats down so he is at eye level with Eira as he rests his arms on the edge of the bathtub. He had entered the room searching for a specific person, but, to his delight, had found something much more valuable.

"Then I'll just—" Eira places her trembling hands on both sides of the bathtub, preparing to pull herself up and out of the large washing basin. It takes all the strength and courage she can muster to move this much. Before she can pull herself up and out, the man halts her by placing a hand on her shoulder.

"Oh, don't get up on my account. You're fine right where you are," he says with a vicious grimace.

The man's hand runs along Eira's shoulder, until it comes across a few stray locks of her black hair, which he takes between his fingers. He shifts his gaze to the inside of the bathtub, his eyes leering across Eira's naked body.

"There must be enough room in here for two, don't you think?"

There is something pure and ancient about the kind of terror this person inspires in her. This is not the kind of fear which guards the realm of discovery and transformation; this is a primitive dread which inspires nothing but agitated horror.

"Just finished washing?" The man leans forwards, taking a whiff of Eira's ebony hair. "That's perfect."

Eira's heart beats with a furious panic, and yet somehow she feels like the blood has stopped moving in her veins. Her muscles have stopped responding to her nervous system's commands, though it does not matter much, since her mind has gone blank with dire anxiety and is in no condition to give orders to her body.

The man leans in further and goes to plant his lips on Eira's neck. Before he makes contact, however, he freezes in place, his face a matter of inches from Eira's.

Both Eira and the rapacious individual turn their gaze upwards. Towering several feet above them is the Archman, who stares down at the man with an intense fury behind his crimson eyes.

CHAPTER Twelve

A THWARTED ADVANCE, PART 2

The man reaches for the handle of his shortsword as fast as he can, but it is a futile effort. The Archman grabs him around the nape of his neck, wraps his large hands around the vital limb, and grips it in a crushing vice.

The man claws at the Archman's fingers, trying to free his neck from the oppressive grasp. The Archman only clutches harder as he slowly lifts the man up single-handedly, letting the man's arms and legs scramble beneath him like a terrified animal trying to escape its predator.

"H-hold on, I—" The man barely manages to squeeze the words out before he is interrupted. The Archman abruptly swings the man's head down, smashing it against the edge of the bathtub.

There is an audible crack accompanied by a spurt of blood, which trickles down the tub into the bathwater. Eira flinches backwards from the sudden strike and instinctively raises her hands to her mouth. Before she can recover from seeing the first blow, the Archman raises the man up once more, then brings his bloodied cranium down onto the bathtub a second time, shattering the man's skull on the hard surface.

The Archman is immolating with an incandescent rage, his scarlet eyes burning vengefully as he devastates his victim in a fit of merciless wrath. Throughout the whole process, he does not make a single sound, but his expression is screaming with malicious intent.

He lifts the man's head one more time but hesitates. He looks down at Eira, who is shivering in the opposite end of the bathtub, as physically far away from the violence as possible. She is still frozen with shock—her only movement an occasional blink.

The Archman closes his eyes and inhales as he gradually composes himself and defuses his temper. He grabs the man by his collar and drags him across the bathroom floor. His victim is thoroughly gored and twitching, leaving a trail of blood as he is hauled out of the bathroom to be extinguished in private.

Eira looks at the edge of the bathtub which had recently been converted into a murder weapon. There are several small dents across the edge, and many more bloodstains to complement the gruesome aesthetic. Though it is a disturbing sight, she ultimately feels relieved, and is now able to take a proper breath for the first time since her assailant entered the room.

The Archman steps back into the room, closing the door and wiping the blood from his hand on his cloak as he walks over to Eira. He stands before the bathtub reluctantly. He wants to look down to check if she is uninjured, but he is hesitant to approach her in her vulnerable state.

"Sorry you had to see that..." He kneels down in front of the bathtub, slowly moving closer towards her with as much pacifism as he can muster.

"It's okay." Eira's voice lilts, as waves of dread continue to ripple through the pond of her psyche.

"Are you okay?" The Archman averts his gaze, facing the same direction as Eira. They are not looking at anything in particular, just avoiding eye contact as much as possible.

"Yeah...I'm fine." She nods, taking a tremulous breath in.

They sit in silence as they are both in a realm which is completely foreign to them. The Archman glances over at Eira and notices her shivering, sitting balled up in the bathtub to conserve as much warmth as possible.

"You should dry off. The water's gone cold," he states plainly.

"Okay..." Eira nods once again. She slowly removes her arms from around her legs and places them on the sides of the bathtub. She tries to lift herself up, but her muscles give out before she can raise herself an inch.

Eira is surprised by how weak she feels, as she has always felt like a powerful, capable person, no more so than when her father was struck ill. She thought she had shown a decent amount of resilience. But just now, presented with something so physically threatening, so immediately traumatising, she realises how frail she really is. It is even more evident when compared to someone like the Archman, who was so unfazed in the face of imminent danger.

The Archman stands up and reaches a hand down, keeping his gaze thoroughly averted. Eira takes his gloved hand in hers and tries to lift herself once again, but to no avail. Her legs feel useless, in fact, more than useless: they feel like nothing but dead weight beneath her.

"I...I can't," she whispers.

The Archman pauses for a second, keeping her hand in his with a soft but firm grip.

"Here." He leans down and lifts Eira's arms up and around his shoulders at the same time, using his upper body as an anchor for her to clutch onto.

"Hold on." The Archman encircles her torso with his arms, then lifts her up and out of the bathtub in one smooth motion. A small amount of cold water follows Eira out of the tub, dripping down onto the floor beneath the two of them.

Eira feels her feet touch the floor and gradually manages to stabilise herself on the solid ground. She clings to the Archman's upper back with her hands for a little longer, as she does not fully trust her legs to hold her up. After a few more seconds she has her sense of balance back, but she still does not let go. Despite being completely naked, she does not feel the slightest bit endangered. She wants to stay like this for just a little while longer. It feels so much easier to breathe with the Archman's arms wrapped around her, and the presence of his body has stopped her shivering completely.

"Can you stand?" the Archman asks at a low volume.

Eira pauses. She does not want to say anything dishonest, but if she tells the truth, he will pull away from her. Instead, she responds by tipping her head forwards, leaning it upon his chest. She holds him tighter, further deepening their contact.

The Archman's eyes widen with a perplexed bewilderment. The only time he has ever been this close to someone was when he was trying to end their life. It feels almost impossible to process what he is experiencing, as he has no frame of reference through which to understand it. Though he cannot recognise exactly what is happening to him, he does not feel the need to cease it prematurely. He follows Eira's cue, holding her with a firmer embrace and leaning his head down so that it is beside hers.

"Sorry...I shouldn't have left," the Archman murmurs, his words muted slightly by his closeness to Eira.

"It's not your fault," Eira says reassuringly, trying to comfort the both of them.

They pull away from one another slowly, savouring the final moments of contact before being separated. Though their hug has officially ended, there is still a bit of warmth lingering inside each of them: inside Eira's stomach and the Archman's chest.

As they fade back into reality, they both become acutely aware of Eira's nakedness. Eira's hands shoot up quickly to cover her breasts as she and the Archman turn away from one another in unison.

"Towel..." the Archman mutters awkwardly as he steps away, looking for the towel they had brought with them. Once he finds it, he brings it and hands it to Eira at arm's length.

"Thanks..." Eira receives the towel and wraps it around herself expeditiously.

"*Sacrebleu!* What's all this?!" Jacob limps down the staircase into the tavern's lobby, surveying the damage all around the vast room. The battle has ended, although its aftermath is still very present in the space. There are pieces of broken furniture everywhere, and the occasional dead body lying about in an eternal laziness. Both the furniture and bodies are being cleaned up by members of the Raeburn crew, some of whom are having their injuries tended to.

"A bunch of bounty hunters." Fiona walks over to Jacob, adjusting the cap on her head, which had been displaced during the brawl. She is covered with random splatters of blood across her body, colouring her gold hair with hints of dark red. Most of the blood is not hers, except for a small amount coming from a shallow wound on her right shoulder, which she is clutching with her left hand. She seems quite unbothered by both the injury and the smattering of human fluids upon her as she makes her way past Jacob to the staircase he descended from.

"I'm going for a bath."

"Yeah, *bonne idée*," Jacob remarks approvingly as he inspects the many bloodstains covering Fiona's skin and clothing.

Fiona is climbing the steps when the Archman and Eira appear at the top of the staircase.

"Ah, *le voilà*. I wondered where you went." Fiona walks up to the Archman with a pleasant smile, which is very much out of alignment with her sanguine outfit.

"How did we manage?" he asks as he looks out across the room.

"*Pas mal.* Thanks for the help." Fiona pats him on the side of his bicep cordially.

The Archman looks down and spots the slice across Fiona's right shoulder. He halts her before she can walk past him.

"They got you?" He points to the laceration that is being partially covered by Fiona's hand.

"Just a little *coupe*. It'll be fine." Fiona waves her hand with a polite dismissal.

The Archman sighs, then turns to walk back upstairs. "Come with me. Let's get you sewn up."

"Oh, really? *Merci.*" Fiona beams as she follows him up the staircase.

Before they leave, the Archman looks back down the staircase at Jacob, pointing down at him with a direct command.

"Also, get back to bed. You shouldn't be on your feet."

"*Je sais, je sais,*" Jacob acknowledges while rolling his eyes and waving his hand with a much less polite dismissal than Fiona.

The Archman turns away and walks back up the stairs, Eira and Fiona in tow. As they ascend, Eira is struck by a sudden impulse, which she immediately acts upon.

"Do you need any help?" she asks courteously.

He looks back at her for a moment, then gives her a quick nod, accompanied by an even quicker smile. "Sure."

FIONA SITS ON THE EDGE OF HER BED, AS THE ARCHMAN finishes cleaning up her gash, being careful not to undo any of the fresh stitches across her shoulder.

"Alright, that'll do it." The Archman wipes the blood from his hands on a bloody rag, then hands it to Eira, who collects it with the several others used throughout the process.

"*Magnifique...*" Fiona looks down at her dressed wound with wonder. She is almost glad to have the injury, as it gave her the opportunity to witness such an elegant display of surgical prowess.

"You can dispose of those." The Archman points to the bloody rags in Eira's possession.

"Right, okay." Eira nods and goes to leave, taking the gory fabrics with her. As she steps out of the bedroom, she catches the end of Fiona's sentence.

"...was a close one. I'm glad you were there."

Eira halts in place outside the room. She is not normally one for eavesdropping, but part of her wants to know how Fiona and the Archman will act in her absence. Another part of her urges her not to spy on their interaction, as she already has an idea of how they might act. Nevertheless, she stays put, in the auditory range of Fiona and the Archman.

"If I hadn't been here, then they wouldn't have come to get me," the Archman rebuts.

"Ah, *c'est vrai.*" Fiona giggles. "But your presence is worth the occasional invasion."

"We'll see if your protection is worth it as well, then."

"*Ne t'inquiète pas,*" Fiona assures him. "You'll get your money's worth."

Though Eira cannot see them, it sounds as though their voices are getting closer and closer together.

"*Merci encore* for the treatment. How did you get so good?" Fiona compliments him with a question.

"Practise. And some trial and error."

Eira cannot resist the urge to bear visual witness to their conversation, as the auditory information is not nearly satisfying enough for snooping purposes. She pokes her head just around the corner of the doorframe and peeks in through the gap from the open door. The Archman is gathering up his surgical instruments; Fiona is hovering at his side.

"*C'est vraiment* amazing work." Fiona looks admiringly at the stitches across her shoulder.

"Thanks," the Archman replies monotonously.

"I feel bad receiving treatment for *gratuit,* though." Fiona puts a hand on the Archman's arm to snare his attention. "I'd love to pay you back, if I could."

"I'll just take a cut off the protection fee," the Archman suggests, not particularly interested in any kind of financial savings.

"Actually, I was thinking of something *d'autre.*" Fiona smiles with a twinkle in her eye.

"Fine, what is it?" The Archman looks down at Fiona with an unvarying expression.

Eira watches with wide eyes as Fiona moves her hand from the Archman's arm to his chest with a smooth motion, then raises herself up on her toes to close the distance between them. She closes her eyes and goes to plant a kiss on his lips, but she is halted before contact can be made. She opens her eyes with surprise, finding the Archman's hand wrapped around her neck. For an initial moment she gives a flustered smile, interpreting it as a playful gesture, but as she looks up at him, her smile quickly disappears.

In a split second, he turns and slams Fiona up against the nearest wall, pinning her in place with a single hand. Her arms shoot up to his wrist as she is consumed by a sudden panic. Eira thought she could not be any more surprised after Fiona's attempted kiss, but this astonishes her much more.

"What do you think you're doing?" The Archman speaks with a cold harshness to his voice. It is a tone which Eira has not heard in quite some time.

"*D-désolé...*" Fiona whimpers fearfully. "I'm sorry...I didn't mean to..."

"I see you're used to taking what you please. Let me make it clear that I won't tolerate that behaviour at all." The Archman unleashes his invective words upon Fiona without a shred of hesitancy.

"*Oui*...okay..." Fiona nods nervously, not deigning to contradict the Archman even the slightest bit in this position.

"This is a professional arrangement. I'd appreciate it if you know your place." He releases his grip on Fiona's throat and she slides down the wall to the ground.

Eira looks at Fiona, who is shaking with petrified uneasiness. It is disquieting seeing such a courageous and unabashed person reduced to a terrified mess.

Eira hastily steps away from the bedroom, absolutely certain that she does not want to be caught. It is hard to believe the person she was embracing just a little while ago is the same one viciously overpowering a woman of relative innocence. Eira wonders how she keeps forgetting that this side of the Archman is his default state.

As she speedily walks away from the bedroom, Eira finds herself experiencing a strange sense of relief, one that is very unbecoming of her current circumstances. Something indicates to her that she would have been much more distressed if the Archman had simply let Fiona kiss him.

CHAPTER Thirteen

A MISPLACED HUNGER, PART 1

"How much longer do you anticipate it will take?" The Archman stands at the edge of the harbour, looking out as dozens of crewmates transport supplies out to four ships resting in the crescent bay.

"A few more hours, *probablement,*" Jacob estimates, observing his subordinates as they take loads of rations and equipment with them in the dinghies, delivering them up to the larger vessels.

Eira waits at the Archman's side, pulling at the collar around her neck, which is starting to heat up under the sun, making it quite uncomfortable against her skin. It is not nearly uncomfortable enough to make it worth bringing up, however, especially since she needs as much social currency with the

Archman as she can gather. She has a certain prospect in mind that she has begun mulling over.

She turns and looks over at Jacob, who is standing upright with a bright freshness. It is an odd state to see him in, as she has only ever engaged with him when he is in a bitter, diseased state. He now looks like a completely different person than he did a week ago: his face has a healthy colour to it, and the dark rings under his eyes are completely gone. His illness is now all but an unpleasant memory.

What amazes Eira the most is how rapid the transformation has been. Jacob already looks ten years younger and it has only been a few days since the Archman's procedure.

Eira had initially surmised that Jacob was Fiona's older brother by a large margin, but now she suspects that he is actually the younger sibling. The additional fact that Fiona is the one currently corralling the crewmates and delegating tasks to them provides more evidence that she is the eldest. Or perhaps it is just a chore she can busy herself with so she can more easily avoid the Archman, something she has been doing a lot more lately.

"*D'ailleurs,* what's our lead going to be?" Jacob asks the Archman, stretching his arms over his head like a plant trying to absorb as much sunlight as possible.

"I'm working on it. The winds have shifted, and the navy could be anywhere," the Archman responds with dry logic. "And we've got bounty hunters to contend with now."

"Ha! Is there *personne* who doesn't want you dead?"

The Archman's eyes glance over at Eira for a split second, then snap back to Jacob.

"Unlikely."

"*Bien*, well, let me know when you've got a lead for us." Jacob gives a final remark before walking away towards Fiona.

The Archman gathers up the chain from Eira's collar, preparing to leave as well. He and Eira walk along one of the many wooden docks, until they arrive at the Archman's dinghy. They climb inside and pull away from the harbour, gliding through the still water towards his ship.

"What's the matter?" the Archman enquires out of nowhere.

"Hmm? What?" Eira quickly sits upright, taken aback by the abrupt question.

"You have a look in your eyes that could pierce steel," the Archman banters casually.

Eira feels her stomach churn uncomfortably, as she is presented with a prime opportunity to act upon the contemplation which has been occupying her.

"It's nothing," Eira says with as much nonchalance as possible so that it seems genuine. The discomfort in her stomach eases but does not go away completely. She knows that she is just putting off an inevitably excruciating conversation, and that she has done nothing more than buy herself time. Part of her wonders if she could just forget about her rumination, but a much larger part of her knows that she would eternally regret it if she did not ask at all.

Eira and the Archman sit in silence all the way back to his ship and stay that way as the dinghy is hoisted up to the platform, as they enter the ship, and as the Archman guides her through the hallways.

The Archman stops before the door to his study. He hands the bundle of chains to Eira, walks inside, and returns a moment later with an empty cloth bag.

“You like making yourself useful, right?” He hands the cloth bag to Eira. “Go to the treasury and fill this with as much as you can carry, then bring it to the dinghy.”

“Oh, sure.” Eira takes the empty bag, sceptical of how much solid gold she will be able to transport while also carrying the bundle of chains.

The Archman steps back into his study, closing the door behind him.

Eira stands with the cloth bag in her hands, caught in an awkward position. Her deliberation would certainly affect the Archman’s plans if she vocalised them, so this is undoubtedly the most crucial time to tell him.

Eira fiddles with the rough fabric of the bag and opts instead to complete the job the Archman has assigned her. She theorises that he would be more receptive to her postulation after she has finished her assigned task, or at least that is what she tells herself, as it gives a plausible excuse to delay the tense conversation once more.

Many hours later, the sun creeps across the sky as it begins its descent towards the western horizon. The Archman’s ship is now in open waters, along with the four other ships that are part of the Raeburn fleet. These vessels would normally stand out against any other boat piloted by the criminally inclined, both in their powerful builds and elegant designs, but as they sail alongside the Archman’s ship, they are nothing more than another bunch of meagre, unassuming watercrafts.

Eira stands with the Archman at the helm of the ship, the aching in her stomach becoming intolerable. Her body is clearly annoyed that she is not speaking up and is chastising her with all manner of corporeal punishments. Eira knows the longer they sail, the harder it will be to voice her thoughts, but she cannot bring herself to form her cogitation into words.

"That'll do for now." The Archman pulls a lever and locks the wheel in place. He walks to the staircase which descends to the main deck; Eira is led along by the slacked chain. He guides her along to the bedroom and opens the door to go inside.

"Go rest now. You don't want to strain your injury too much," he instructs.

Eira looks into the bedroom, the gnawing in her stomach only worsening as her window of opportunity is about to slam shut for an indefinite amount of time.

The Archman looks down at her, his eyes narrowing as her unusually tense behaviour has become too outlandish to ignore.

"What's going on?" he says with an interrogative angle. "Are you ill?"

"No, I'm fine," Eira says with a forced half-smile.

"Are you?"

Eira pauses tersely, a bead of sweat rolling down the back of her neck.

"Well...I..." She keeps her eyes focused on the inside of the bedroom, using it as an excuse not to make eye contact.

"That procedure you did worked so well on Jacob." Eira grabs her right wrist with her left hand, feeling a compulsive need to occupy her hands.

"I appreciate it, but what does he have to do with this?" The Archman tilts his head slightly.

"You're an expert on mortal diseases, right?"

"There's still much I don't understand. But compared to your barbaric practices, I suppose so."

"Then...um..." Eira murmurs trepidatiously. "You could theoretically help anyone?"

"Who are we talking about?" the Archman questions with a heavy suspicion.

"My..." Eira hesitates, taking a full breath before going any further. "...my father."

The Archman stands by silently, starting to piece together what Eira is circuitously asking of him. He looks around, feeling a desire for privacy despite the fact they are the only ones on the ship.

"Here." He pushes Eira into the bedroom, closing the door most of the way behind them and leaving it ajar just enough to let in some sunlight.

"What does your father have to do with this?" The Archman crosses his arms, his scepticism evolving into a heavy dubiousness.

"I...nothing, really. I just..." Eira's mind is racing, making it all the more difficult to enunciate her words.

"You just what?" The Archman's patience is beginning to thin.

"I was wondering if you could help him." Eira crosses her arms over her stomach, which immediately soothes itself the moment the words leave her mouth.

The Archman takes a moment to receive her request, his features not shifting at all as he ponders, making it impossible to discern his thoughts.

"Help him," he repeats.

"He's been ill for several years now. We've tried everything, but it's only gotten worse."

"And you want me to cure him?" the Archman clarifies.

"If you could..." Eira says softly, still ardently averting her gaze.

"Let me make sure I understand you correctly..." The Archman straightens his posture, adding another inch to his already sizeable height.

"You want me to travel to this father of yours with the navy and innumerable bounty hunters on our trail, and then stay put long enough for me to diagnose and cure him?" An irritated indignation starts to grow around the Archman's words, slowly spreading out to possess his body as well.

"But you have the Raeburn's protection now, don't you?"

"My point exactly. You're asking to not only put my life, but their lives on the line as well." The Archman steps forward, closing in on Eira's space. She steps back with a pang of agitation, finding her back up against a wall.

"You're asking me to stick my neck out to save someone who I have no affiliation with, someone who I don't even know, and for what? What could you possibly offer me in return? I healed Jacob in exchange for his protection. I'm not a charity." The Archman's brow furrows into a temperamental pattern.

"I...I just thought—" Eira feels her lips start to quiver with distress, as a creeping regret starts burgeoning inside her.

"You thought wrong, princess." His words start to heat with a kindling anger.

"I don't know what inspired you to make such an outrageous demand. Clearly you forget which of us is on the end of the leash." The Archman holds up the bundle of chains to further drive his point forwards. "It's already hard enough to have you around. And now you want to place yet another burden on me?"

"Am I that much of an impediment?" Eira glances up at the Archman, tears starting to line the corners of her eyes.

"An impediment? No, much worse. A distraction." The Archman leans in close to Eira and places a hand on the wall beside her head, closing her in further. He does not let her look away as his vermillion eyes glare deep into her light hazel ones.

"You forget what I am, Eira." He raises his other hand up, taking a firm hold of her chin, his large grasp reaching all the way back to her left ear. Eira flinches from the sudden contact as a fervent panic starts to overtake her.

"You are human. My prey. Having you prancing about my ship is like having a rich delicacy sitting right before you which you are unable to taste no matter how powerfully the impulse strikes. And let me tell you, the impulse strikes often."

Eira is shivering all over from the Archman's constricting position. She wants to open her mouth to apologise, desperate to defuse the situation in any way possible. Unfortunately, the Archman's hand makes it quite impossible.

"But you know what?" He leans in even closer, shrinking the distance between them to a matter of inches. "You made an excellent point. With the Raeburn's protection, I'm now able to fend off that fiancé of yours with much more ease."

Eira looks into the Archman's ruby-red eyes and sees her own petrified reflection in them.

"So tell me...what use do I have for you now?" The Archman's words carry a deathly weight to them. "I needed you as collateral before. But that is no longer a necessity. So what value do you have to me now?" The Archman steps closer, moving his hand off the wall, down to Eira's arm as he pins her against the vertical wooden surface behind her.

Even if she were free of his grasp, escape would be challenging as her legs have lost their ability to function. She feels a growing fear seize her chest, but something about this frightfulness is unusual. She cannot describe it with words, but for some reason, it does not feel like all hope is lost.

The Archman opens his mouth, baring his two razor-sharp fangs, which hang right in front of Eira's face like a pair of foreboding knives. His eyes lower down to her neck with a carnivorous energy.

"I've had to stare at that enticing neck of yours for over a month. I felt like I was dying of thirst. But today, that comes to an end."

The Archman forcibly tilts her head to the side, exposing her sun-kissed neck. There is a ravenous look in his eyes. Eira only manages to catch a glimpse of it before he leans in slowly.

Eira shudders as she feels the Archman place his lips upon her neck. There is a familiar paradox to them, as their surface has a distinct coldness to them, despite the presence of a burning heat behind several layers of skin. The Archman's fangs graze against her skin, causing her eyes to widen with shock. The fangs press lightly against her jugular, with the slightest amount of pressure. All it would take is a bit of extra force, and they would be deep inside her neck. Eira closes her eyes and waits for the sharp impaling sensation that would soon meet her.

For some reason, that moment does not come. For several seconds, the fangs just sit upon the surface of her skin, waiting for the command from their master. Eira can feel the Archman's body shift strangely against hers, like he is trying to adjust his stance. Eventually she feels the fangs lose contact with her skin, as he pulls away from her neck.

Eira opens her eyes and looks up at him, trying to comprehend what is going on. He is looking down at her with a deeply quizzical look, blinking several times. He is evidently just as confused as she is. Something about this just does not feel quite right to him. It is close to the right thing, but it is just a bit off.

The Archman looks into her eyes for a suspended moment, both sharing in the moment of perplexity. The paralysing distress which had seized Eira suddenly starts to loosen its grip. The deathly gaze in the Archman's eyes starts to melt away, but the voraciousness behind them stays firmly in place. Not only does it persist, but it starts to grow.

He drops his eyes back down, but this time his glance lands on her lips.

CHAPTER Fourteen

A MISPLACED HUNGER, PART 2

The Archman leans into Eira once again, both of them instinctively shutting their eyes as the space between them slowly closes into nothing. He places his lips upon Eira's with a firm softness. The moment of initial contact seems to freeze in time, burning itself deep into their memories.

There is a crackling of energy between the two of them as they both lean further into the kiss.

It takes Eira a moment to recuperate from the whiplash of experiences that she has just gone through. Just a few seconds ago she was genuinely fearing for her life, and now she feels more alive than she ever knew possible.

It feels like the Archman's lips have a magical quality to them. Eira had only ever used a kiss as a polite greeting with a close relative, or as a sign of affection towards her parents, and it never trespassed anywhere outside their cheek. It had not occurred to Eira that the simple gesture could be so inherently erotic. This kiss sends shivers of bliss throughout her whole nervous system, warming her from the inside out.

The Archman takes hold of her chin once again, tilting her face upwards slightly to give him greater access to her lips. From this proximity, she can easily pick up on his natural aroma. It has a rich, primordial quality to it which she cannot compare to any other scent she knows. It is such a simple stimulus, but it affects Eira in ways that she cannot describe.

A soft lilt of delight escapes her mouth between pecks, but it is cut off ever so slightly as the Archman quickly re-establishes contact between the two of them. As if to offer a response to her light moan, a faint growl of elation breaks free of the Archman's lips. While there are no words spoken between them, they understand one another completely, as they communicate in the oldest, most universal language known to humankind.

Just when Eira thinks she is acclimating to the Archman's exhilarating kisses, he takes the interaction one level higher, sliding his tongue into Eira's mouth with a presumptive invitation.

Eira jolts slightly from the sudden connection. She had always assumed there was only enough room in her mouth for her own tongue, but the Archman clearly proved her wrong. She is now well outside her realm of familiarity where kissing is concerned. In spite of that, she can easily acquaint herself with this new form of physical engagement. It makes her heart race with a kind of excitement impossible to recreate in any other circumstance.

The Archman's body takes an unconscious cue from his lips and moves closer to Eira, pressing his chest and midriff upon her. By using his large frame to pin her to the wall, his hands are given liberty to explore. He places a palm on the left side of her torso as his fingers slowly close onto her body. He starts with a light touch at first, but it quickly grows in its firmness as he caresses the side of her body, down to her waist.

Eira's back arches reflexively from his touch. It sends sparks of ecstasy all throughout her, which slowly starts collecting in her lower abdomen. It feels like a fire is being ignited inside her stomach, the flames of which crack and spurt as the Archman drags his fingers across her and kisses her with a consuming passion.

It is such an intense sensation that she is not sure how much longer she will be able to withstand it. At the same time, she does not want the feeling to come to an end. It keeps growing and developing into something new as the Archman touches her just a little harder and kisses her just a little more vigorously.

Eira slowly slides her hands up his back, pulling him closer to her. She is unsure if it is an appropriate action to take but given that the Archman acquainted their tongues without hesitation, this much would certainly be acceptable. The Archman reciprocates the action by placing his hand on the small of her back, pulling her towards him so they are even closer.

Eira has never wanted this from someone before. She never really demands much from others to begin with, a trait that she often prides herself on. This is the first time she feels an honest, unabashed selfishness.

She had been able to ignore her nocturnal fantasies easily enough, brushing them off as inconsequential nightly musings. Now that she has gotten a taste of that fantasy, however, it will be impossible to deny how powerfully it compels her. She wants the Archman like nothing she has ever wanted before.

Suddenly, Eira is snapped out of her reverie of physical glee as the Archman pulls away from her with a cruel abruptness. He places his hands on both her shoulders and pushes her away, separating them by an arm's length. Eira opens her eyes with a distraught confusion. She looks up at the Archman, her immediate thought being a dreaded concern that she overstepped some kind of boundary.

The look on the Archman's face seems to suggest that it is something else entirely. He is wracked by a fraught dismay, like he has just ripped himself out of a deep trance. A horrified bewilderment overtakes him as he lets go of Eira and takes several steps backwards. Eira has never seen him in such a fearful state. It seems like the only mortal creature that can possibly inspire such terror inside him is himself.

Eira recoils against the wall, unsure what she should say, if anything at all.

"I..." the Archman mutters to no one in particular, looking away from Eira as he tries to compose himself. He glances back at her for a brief moment, just long enough to see her cheeks flushed with a bright, rosy excitement.

He quickly averts his gaze again and pulls the hood of his cloak over his head as he makes for the door. He swings it open and slams it violently behind him as he exits.

Eira places her hands against the wall behind her to steady herself and to find her balance in the now pitch-black room. Everything had happened so fast, she is beginning to doubt whether it really occurred. This is certainly the strangest she has ever seen the Archman behave.

While she certainly enjoyed that brief moment of unbridled passion, its obscure conclusion has left a strange taste in her mouth, or perhaps that is just the faint hint of the Archman's saliva lingering on her tongue.

Either way, this certainly was not how she was anticipating the interaction would play out. She had gotten a pretty clear refusal to her request initially, but the Archman's actions after the fact did not seem to correlate to his refusal. Eira wishes she could get a clearer answer, but she does not want to push the issue any further.

The door opens back up with a sudden swing as the Archman enters the room with the same urgency with which he left. He retrieves the slacked chain attached to Eira's collar and quickly gathers it up in silence. He looks down at his work, not acknowledging Eira's presence at all.

"Um—" Eira starts.

"Let's go," the Archman says curtly, pulling on the chain, causing Eira to lurch forwards. It has been a while since he has handled her with such a gruff lack of tactfulness.

"W-wait, where are we—"

"The brig, where you belong." The Archman leads Eira out of the bedroom, his back firmly turned away from her.

"Hold on!" Eira grabs the chain, trying to resist the Archman's commandeering in a manner which is beyond futile. He continues to drag her along single-handedly, towards the hatch leading below decks.

"*Archomme!* Hey, *Archomme!*" Jacob's voice cuts across the water, quickly reaching Eira and the Archman, who both turn around to face the direction of his voice.

Jacob and Fiona's ship has sailed up beside the Archman's. Jacob is standing at the edge of his ship, clearly trying to get his attention. The Archman pulls Eira along with him sternly as he walks over to the edge of his ship so that he can speak with Jacob without needing to yell.

"What? I'm busy," the Archman says dismissively.

"You're about to get a lot busier." Jacob raises his voice slightly to cross the space between the two of their ships. He points back, past the stern of their ships. "We've got ourselves some *compagnie.*"

Eira and the Archman lean over the edge of the banister, looking behind them. In the near distance, six vessels are approaching in a quasi-organised manner. They do not appear to be naval vessels, but that does little to ease everyone's rapidly rising concerns.

"Privateers," the Archman says with a cold stillness.

"*Tout le monde* wants a piece of you," Jacob says with a nervous smile.

"We can *probablement* outpace them if we go full sails." Fiona walks up beside Jacob, sliding midway into the conversation.

"I was thinking the same thing." Jacob nods in agreement.

The Archman looks back at the approaching ships, recognising the inherent danger they present, but seeing a different opportunity afforded by their arrival. His brow furrows with a vicious concentration, finding several subjects upon which he can inflict his newfound confusions.

"No." The Archman turns to Jacob and Fiona, the ferocious intensity still very much present in his glare. "Get yourselves armed and ready. At my command, we'll turn about and face them head-on."

Jacob and Fiona pause in a moment of discombobulated hesitation. They are caught in an awkward position, not wanting to engage in a senseless battle if it can be avoided, but, also, neither of them wishing to contradict the Archman.

"Err, *mais*...is that wise?" Jacob suggests as diplomatically as he can.

"Probably not. Be ready in five minutes," the Archman orders, turning and leaving curtly.

Jacob and Fiona watch in addled confusion as the Archman exits the conversation promptly, with Eira in tow.

"Here. Stay put." The Archman hands the bundle of chains off to Eira, who receives the mass of metal links in an awkward fashion.

"Ah, but—" Before Eira can get a word in, the Archman is gone, disappearing below decks at a crucial pace.

Eira slowly gathers up the mess of chain links, which have fallen into a slovenly lump of uncoordinated metal rings. By the time she has assembled everything together, the Archman is exiting from below decks. He is donning his combat attire: pistols, sash, and silver rapier all included.

Under any other circumstance, Eira would have taken a moment to admire the flattering getup, but the current atmosphere hardly gives rise to that option.

"Come." The Archman takes Eira by her arm and pulls her to the bedroom. She would have resisted at least a little if she had not been weighted down by several pounds of chain. Fortunately, her mouth is still quite free to use.

"Wait, can we just stop for a moment?!" she protests, still being led along by her arm.

"Now's hardly the time," the Archman responds brusquely.

"Why are you doing this?!" Eira objects fervently as he opens the bedroom door and shoves her into the dark space.

"Stay here. Don't leave until I come to get you," he instructs with an irrefutable energy. "Understand?"

"No! I don't understand at all!" Eira says with rising vexation. "What has possessed you?!"

"Hellspawn can't be possessed. You should know that," the Archman deflects tersely. "It's going to be dangerous. Stay put."

He slams the door shut, leaving Eira without a shred of light to help her navigate her surroundings. He ascends the staircase to the upper deck and advances to the steering wheel. He turns all the cranks until the ship's sails have been retracted, then pulls a lever to drop the anchor, quickly slowing the ship down.

He then moves to the side of the ship and looks down over the edge at Fiona and Jacob's ship, which rests a few feet down and away from his own.

"Ready?" he calls out from above with a boisterous voice.

"*Presque!*" Jacob replies quickly, moving about at a frantic pace with the rest of the crew.

"Good. May I come aboard?"

"Huh? *Oui.*"

The Archman steps up onto the banister and leaps over the edge, landing on the upper deck of Fiona and Jacob's ship with a heavy but graceful impact. He rises to a standing position and looks out at the vessels coming towards them, now significantly closer.

"*Donc*, how are we going to engage?" Jacob looks out at the same view as the Archman and skittishly runs a hand through his short blonde hair.

The Archman stares down the oncoming ships, mentally preparing himself for the inevitable grim encounter. His face is locked in a gaze of deathly intent.

"Get as close as you can."

CHAPTER Fifteen

AN EXPOSED WOUND, PART 1

A crisp breeze carries Fiona and Jacob's ship towards their oncoming foes. Their three other allied ships follow closely on either side. There is a palpable tension in the air as the crew hold their positions on their vessels, each of them armed with cutlasses or pistols; some of the men are in charge of manning a cannon.

The Archman stands at the very front of the ship; his hands are balled into fists on either side of him. He looks out towards the six approaching vessels, his gaze locking onto them with a deadly fixation. There is a wide empty space around him, as everyone onboard keeps their distance from him. Even then, the crew can still feel the bloodlust emanating from the Archman. Though he does not provide the most pleasant company, many of the crewmates are glad to have him on their side.

“Everything ready?” The Archman turns around, walking towards Jacob with a direct stride.

“Ah, *oui.* All ready.” Jacob gives a hesitant thumbs-up, followed by a disingenuous smile.

“Good.” The Archman walks past Jacob briskly but stops and turns back as a final thought comes to mind. “Tell your crew to stay out of my way.”

“*Absolument.*” Jacob agrees as quickly as possible, nodding at least five times in quick succession.

The Archman walks up to the centre mast of the ship. Crewmates clear a path for him as he walks forward, his radius of lethality thoroughly warding them off. He takes hold of a network of ropes and starts climbing up the rigging until he is most of the way up the mast. He hangs from this heightened position with a single gloved hand, looking out from his vantage point at the advancing ships. Tensions continue to grow as everyone collectively holds their breath.

“AT THE READY!!!” Fiona bellows from the stern of the ship, where she is steering.

There is a lulled silence as the two small fleets of ships draw closer and closer, until the crews of each craft become visible to one another. An approaching ship starts to pass by on the port side of Fiona and Jacob’s vessel. The crew immediately gather themselves on the starboard side of the ship, distancing themselves from their foes. With weapons drawn, the crew’s nerves are heightened.

There is a reluctant pause, as no one dares make the first move. This hesitation is broken abruptly as a beckoning command comes from the oncoming ship.

“ADVANCE!!!”

The mob of privateers lay down a series of gangplanks and start swarming onto the vessel, blades and firearms drawn.

The Archman grabs a rope from the rigging beside him, and swings through the air in an acrobatic stunt which catches the attention of both allies and enemies. He lands before the advancing horde with a heavy impact, catching them severely off guard. He slowly raises to a standing position as the unprepared privateers all turn and look at him in fascinated terror.

The Archman draws his rapier in one hand and a single pistol in the other and surveys his soon-to-be victims.

"IT'S HIM!!!" A frenetic voice blurts out from the mob of armed privateers.

The sudden burst of noise shatters the stillness like a veil of thin ice, causing the privateers to rush at the Archman en masse, brandishing their weapons. Some of them assume a vicious war cry.

The Archman responds with a cold ferocity, pulling back the hammer on his pistol and picking off the closest target before him. Then, with his rapier, he cuts into the next closest body to approach him.

After the first body hits the floor, everything in the Archman's vision starts to blur into a dark crimson hue. He is consumed with a deluge of ruthlessness as he fends off and cuts down his attackers with expert movements. Flesh is parred and pierced on the edge of his glistening blade as his pistol picks off targets one at a time with deadly efficiency. Cries of gore ring out as the massacre unfolds, but the Archman is completely deaf to the sounds around him, as all his senses limit themselves to the bare necessities of survival and savagery. Bodies fall off him like he is brushing water from his skin. One can sense the carnage that he is radiating without even needing to look at him. Musket balls collide against his body every now and then, but they are stopped dead in their tracks by the fortified leather and fabric of his combat attire. They leave nothing behind but irritable bruises and have little effect other than further stoking the Archman's fury.

Jacob and Fiona's crew rush in to retaliate, adding further to the bloodied frenzy. Streams of red coat the deck like a grim painting upon a wooden canvas.

A single opportunistic privateer attacks the Archman from a blind spot, swinging down at him with a cutlass. The blade cuts into the Archman's shoulder, just barely making it through his armoured jacket and digging slightly into his flesh.

The Archman winces in pain and lets out a stifled groan. He whips around instantly and grabs his attacker by the wrist, pulling him closer and driving his rapier through the man's gut. The man lurches over and screams in agony as the Archman grabs his victim by the base of his hair. Without a moment of hesitation, the Archman opens his mouth and swings his head down, burying his fangs deep into the man's neck. The man suddenly stops screaming as he feels the life being extracted out of him.

The Archman withdraws his fangs once the man stops twitching, dropping the fresh corpse to the ground. He looks back up, his mouth and chest painted with red carnage, matching the colour of his blade. All around him, the privateers have halted their assault, as it has become clear that approaching the deathly being before them produces an irrefutably fatal result.

With no one daring to come close, the Archman pulls the hammer back on his pistol and lifts his blade as he walks forwards. It was now his turn to take the offence.

MEANWHILE, EIRA SITS ON THE EDGE OF THE BED IN THE bedroom back on the Archman's ship. She has the door wide open so she is not senselessly waiting in the dark, although she had considered closing it, as a completely shrouded darkness most accurately reflects her current mood.

She is trying not to use the ample amount of time to overthink everything, though it is proving to be a losing battle. What preoccupies her more than anything is the knowledge that the Archman is currently engaging in a battle of his own, one which certainly carries higher stakes than Eira's.

Even though she has seen the Archman's uncontested combat prowess before, she cannot help but worry. A plaguing thought keeps nagging her, asking what would happen if by some chance the Archman were not to return from this skirmish.

Eira feels a certain kind of bitter anger that she is unable to assist in any possible way. Just as was the case with her father, she is powerless to help the Archman. The only difference in this circumstance is that the Archman clearly did not want her support, and for some reason, that bothers her more than anything else.

The clunk of footsteps snaps her attention upwards. She walks to the doorway slowly, making sure the footsteps are from a friendly source before taking any further action. She is relieved to see Fiona and Jacob, accompanied by several crewmates, walking across the deck of the Archman's ship. They are behind the Archman, barely able to keep up with him.

Eira's relief proves to be quite short-lived. The Archman clutches his left shoulder with one hand as he limps along, a trail of blood following him across the deck. Fiona and Jacob look to be speaking to the Archman in a fervent panic, but his body language clearly indicates that he is dismissing whatever they are saying. He opens the hatch to go below decks and disappears with Fiona and Jacob in tow.

Eira quickly exits the bedroom and follows them below decks, trying to catch up as best she can while being weighed down by several pounds of chain. She follows the trail of blood down the stairs to the bottom level of the ship, then to the end of the hallway, where Fiona and Jacob are standing trepidatiously. They are standing outside the laboratory–slaughterhouse, a pensive energy being shared by the two of them.

"Is he in there?" Eira asks as she approaches them.

"Yeah." Jacob nods.

"Is he okay?" Eira enquires urgently.

"He seems to think so," Fiona comments ambiguously.

Eira walks up to the closed door, places a hand on it, and pauses for a moment. She is not sure what she will be engaging with on the other side of the door, but she knows it is not to be taken lightly.

"He asked us not to go in," Fiona informs her cautiously.

"You might want to stay back, then," Eira suggests as she pushes open the door and walks inside. She steps inside the laboratory–slaughterhouse as the door closes quickly behind her.

Eira squints through the dim lamplight and sees the Archman sitting upon the steel table in the centre of the room. His heavy leather jacket and white undershirt have been removed and set aside, leaving the Archman completely shirtless. He is holding a needle and thread between his hands, fiddling with them in a frustrated state.

When he spots Eira, he immediately drops the needle and thread, grabs his white undershirt and pulls it over across his upper body with a flustered anger.

"I didn't say you could enter!" he barks angrily, adjusting the shirt to cover as much exposed flesh as possible.

"Unlike you, I don't feel the need to ask every time," Eira asserts as she walks towards him, setting the bundle of chains down on the metal table.

"I told you to stay upstairs," the Archman rebuts with a scathing tone.

"Are you okay?" Eira ignores his abrasive words and slowly steps closer.

"I'm fine." The Archman looks away with a stern frown. There is something almost childish about his deliberately curt nature. The juvenile image does not align with his appearance, however, as his mouth and neck are awash with a fresh layer of sanguine liquid. The blood on his left shoulder leaks onto the white shirt, making his testimony of good health hard to believe.

"Why did you do that?" Eira asks plainly, letting her genuine curiosity shine through.

"Do what?" The Archman keeps his gaze sternly averted.

"All of this. Was it really necessary? Jacob and Fiona said we could have just escaped without a fight."

"They would've kept chasing us. Better to deal with the problem right away."

Eira closes her eyes and exhales audibly. She shifts her attention to the quickly growing bloodstain on his shoulder.

"You're hurt."

"Thanks. I hadn't noticed," the Archman scoffs sardonically.

"Let me see." Eira reaches for the fabric of the shirt, once again ignoring his harsh tone.

"I can handle it myself, thanks." The Archman swats Eira's hand away.

"Really? For someone with so much anatomical knowledge, you should know that it's quite impossible to stitch a wound you can't see," Eira rebukes.

The Archman sits in silence, recognising that she is correct, but the last thing he wants to do is admit it.

"I've got some sewing experience. It's not exactly the same, but I'm sure it's applicable." Eira continues her line of reasoning as she picks up the needle and thread from the table.

The Archman remains in his silent state, struggling to come up with a counter-argument. He is not exactly in the ideal headspace to be debating.

"I'll be careful. I promise," Eira says reassuringly, defusing the contentious nature of their conversation. She slowly reaches for the white undershirt, but the Archman grabs her wrist to halt her for a moment. Behind his unflinching expression, there is a twinge of nervousness, or perhaps something even more profound.

"Just...keep your eyes on your work," the Archman says with significantly less volume.

Eira nods in a comforting manner, then slowly pulls the white shirt off his upper body. He lets it slip off him with a tense timidness.

CHAPTER Sixteen

AN EXPOSED WOUND, PART 2

Eira is immediately taken aback by what she sees but hides it as best she can. Almost every inch of the Archman's chest, torso, back, shoulders, and arms are covered in scars, all of which vary heavily in size, depth, severity, and age. It seems almost impossible for one person to have accumulated so many lesions, although if someone had dozens of lifetimes to do so, it certainly could be plausible.

Eira decides not to make any comments, as the Archman looks visibly uncomfortable in his shirtless state. She can empathise with him in that regard, but he evidently has much more reason to be insecure than she does.

Eira takes the needle and thread and steps around behind him, threading the thin strand through the miniscule eye of the needle. Once prepared, she wipes away as much blood as she can with the shirt, then focuses on the open wound on the back of his shoulder. It is a slash about two inches long, which fortunately does not go too deep. She places a hand beside the lesion to steady herself, then brings the needle close to the damaged flesh.

The Archman grunts lightly as she inserts the small metal instrument into his skin.

"Sorry..." she whispers.

"It's fine," he says in a neutral tone.

"Do you want something to bite down on?"

"I think I've bitten enough things for today." The Archman wipes away some of the blood from around his mouth.

"Thanks for sparing my neck, at least," Eira says lightheartedly, hoping to ease some of the discomfort as she sews together his wound.

"Well, that wasn't the plan," he replies without the same humorous bent to his words.

"What was the plan then?" Eira enquires, her eyes drifting towards the Archman's face every now and then.

"I don't know...I mean, I thought I had one. You've made it quite challenging to concoct any sort of objective."

"I know, I'm a distraction, correct?"

"At first, perhaps, but you've become so much worse." The Archman's voice tremors ever so slightly.

"What's worse than a distraction?" Eira stops closing up the wound, as she cannot consistently keep her attention on it.

"A contradiction. That's what you are."

"Am I?" she asks with a restrained curiosity.

The Archman freezes, clearly struggling to formulate his thoughts into words. It is the first time Eira has seen him tongue-tied.

"Like right now. Why the hell are you treating my injury?"

"I can't just leave it like this," she replies simply.

The Archman turns his head towards her, suddenly overtaken by an agitated tension. "But why?! I already told you I won't help your father! What other reason could you possibly have?!"

"I owe you at least this much. You saved my life, after all."

"I saved your life because you're more valuable to me alive than dead," the Archman refutes.

"Well..."— Eira hesitates for a brief moment, looking away from him—"...you're more valuable to me alive as well."

The Archman looks back at Eira, his face plastered with a profound confusion, accompanied by a faint lightness.

"This is what I mean..." He returns his gaze forwards. "You make no sense. I'm your captor! I'm the Archman! You should want me dead!"

"You hardly make any sense yourself. I'm meant to be your prisoner..." Eira feels her face redden as she speaks. "...so why did you kiss me?"

"I..." The Archman lowers his gaze, struggling to come up with an answer. "Please just forget about that."

"Forget it?" Eira feels a sudden tightness in her chest.

"What happened between us...it's not right," he explains with a significant challenge. His whole body is quaking with an agitated energy, which is barely being contained. "It's not what I do. I collect you, I dissect you, I consume you. That's what I do."

"Then why haven't you consumed me already?"

"I DON'T KNOW!!!" The Archman slams a fist down on the metal table, leaving behind a small dent. He is seething through his blood-soaked teeth, his breathing shallow and stagnant.

"I don't know, okay?" He runs a hand up through his silver hair, closing his eyes with an exhausted sigh. "I just...I don't want to."

A calm silence fills the space after being briefly displaced.

"That's a relief, I suppose..." Eira goes back to mending the wound, pulling the thread through the lacerated flesh to close the gash. She keeps her left palm on his shoulder to steady herself, once again sensing the anomalous temperature of his skin: a thin layer of cold on the surface, with a profound heat lying just beneath. It reminds Eira of his lips, which carry the same incongruous property. She wonders if the rest of his body is similar.

"Your father..." the Archman speaks up, barely above a whisper, but slowly getting louder with each word. "...what is it that ails him?"

Eira pauses her sewing, taken slightly aback by the enquiry. She quickly returns to her work, trying not to appear as surprised as she really is.

"We think it's the white plague. He's been coughing up blood for months now."

"What state was he in when you last saw him?"

"It wasn't good...he was quite sickly. He could hardly walk." Eira's voice quivers ever so slightly as she recalls her father's plight. She has been so preoccupied with her own immediate survival the past while that she had forgotten how close to death he was.

"How can you be certain that he's even alive?" the Archman presses further.

Eira hesitates for a moment, ceasing her sewing work, as her hands have begun to tremor.

"I don't...he may very well be gone by now." Eira tries to stabilise her hands, but their unconscious twitching only seems to grow worse. The thought of her father passing is disturbing enough, but then she considers how her mother might react. It would be an absolutely crushing occurrence: losing her only daughter to a cruel abduction, then having her husband succumb to illness.

Eira feels a dampness accumulating in the corners of her eyes as she imagines the torment her parents are going through in her absence. She raises the back of her hand to her face, desperately fighting back the urge to cry as her breathing hitches sporadically.

The Archman looks back at her for a brief moment, then turns back away.

"Sorry...I shouldn't have asked," he apologises.

"It's fine." Eira takes a sharp breath in, composing herself enough to finish treating the Archman's wound. She ties off the thread and clips it with a pair of scissors laying on the metal table.

"There...that should do it."

The Archman quickly takes his white shirt and returns it to his upper body, buttoning it up to shelter the dozens of cicatrices across his skin. Eira catches a few final glimpses before he pulls the bloodstained fabric over his body. She tries to imagine how many misfortunes must have befallen him to have collected so many lesions.

"Thank you..." He stands up from the table as he buttons up the rest of his shirt, still averting his gaze from Eira.

"It's nothing."

The Archman puts on his leather gloves and takes the jacket off the table. Eira follows suit, gathering up the bundle of chains in both arms. They both make their way to the door without another word between them.

They step out into the corridor, where Jacob and Fiona are loitering. They quickly stand up to attention as they see the Archman exit the room with Eira.

"Ah, *ça va*?" Fiona enquires trepidatiously, keeping a generous distance from him.

"Yes." The Archman strides past Jacob and Fiona, who quickly scramble to catch up with him. Eira has to quicken her pace considerably to keep up as well.

"*Alors*...should we just keep our course?" Jacob leans forward to try and catch the Archman's attention.

The Archman suddenly halts in place, forcing everyone else to stop along with him. His face is frozen in a state of deep pondering, as he consults and grapples with Jacob's question with much effort.

"No." He comes to a conclusion, exhaling some of his tension.

"*D'accord,* so where are we headed?" Jacob asks.

The Archman turns around and faces Eira. "Where is your estate?"

"What?" She straightens her posture as everyone's attention suddenly turns to her.

"*Attendez,* wait. Where are we going?" Fiona questions in an abrasive tone.

"I have an errand to run," the Archman asserts definitively, leaving no room for recourse or debate.

He turns back to Eira. "Where does your family live?"

A FEW BEAMS OF SUNLIGHT BREAK THROUGH THE GREY, overcast sky, washing everything in dull monochrome shades. Eira stands on the main deck next to one of the large masts, a bucket of soapy water in her hands. She lathers the soap onto the mast with an overused rag.

She looks up at the clouded sky, searching for any indication that it may come to an end. They have been plagued with this weather quite consistently for the past three days or so, though the lack of sunlight seems to be a preference for the Archman, so Eira does not mind it all that much.

Her gaze falls towards the port they are currently docked in. It is the same one Eira had departed from with Normond over a month ago. The Archman's oversized ship takes up nearly two spaces in the port but given that it is currently the only vessel docked there, it is inconsequential.

She turns her sights to the open water, where she can faintly see the ships of Fiona and Jacob's crew in the distance. Each is spread out miles and miles from one another to form a kind of monitored perimeter around the Archman's ship.

The Archman steps up out of the lower deck, a cloth bag slung over his shoulder and a rapier secured to his left hip, covered slightly by his black cloak. He walks over to Eira, unlocks the chain from around the mast, collects up the slack, and turns towards her. She eyes the rapier at his hip with a tense gaze.

"It's a precautionary measure. I won't use it unless I have to," the Archman explains. "Let's go."

Eira walks in tow with him, moving as quickly as she can without overtaking him. She had grown increasingly antsy to leave the ship and return to her parents, but it is clear that her status on this vessel is still little more than a dignified prisoner.

Eira and the Archman descend a steep ramp to reach the dock, the length of chain and the contents of the Archman's cloth bag clanking with every one of his paces.

"Is that the way?" He points to a dirt road which leads out of the port, stretching out into the imperceptible distance.

"Yes, just down the road." Eira nods.

"Is it a long walk?" He starts towards the road; Eira follows beside him.

"I—Actually, I don't know. I've never walked it before."

"I suppose Her Majesty isn't used to such a lowly method of travel," the Archman quips in a lighthearted tone.

Eira feels her heart flutter for half a second. It has been the first time he has made a jest regarding her noble background since their contentious interaction. Ordinarily she might have retaliated with a backhanded remark of her own, but she is content enough just seeing a glimpse of his playful nature.

It is an otherwise uneventful promenade towards Eira's homestead, but once her property comes into view, Eira can feel a heavy tension slowly starting to seize her. It starts with just a knot in her stomach but gradually spreads to her chest and shoulders.

Her latent urgency makes her walk much faster than usual, placing her on par with the Archman's normal marching speed. They walk up the stone path to the front doors. There are still no signs of human activity, though it is not like there was ever a lot to begin with. And with this kind of weather, the servants would all be staying inside.

By the time they arrive before the front doors, the tightness in Eira's body has become a debilitating rigidity, making it hard to do even the simplest of bodily functions. She is not sure what she will encounter on the other side of the doors. She has already conceived of many potential worst-case scenarios, most of which concocted themselves against her will.

Eira's dithering is quickly interrupted as the Archman slams his fist on one of the doors several times, knocking with much more force than necessary. After a few seconds of silence, a faint movement is heard from behind the door. Latches are turned and unlocked, then the doorknob turns a quarter-circle in a clockwise manner.

The Archman stands behind Eira with a looming energy. Though his appearance does not exactly inspire security, Eira feels comforted being in his presence. She takes a sharp breath in, steeling herself for whatever circumstance will present itself.

CHAPTER Seventeen

A STRINGENT EXAMINATION

The faded white door pulls away from its frame slowly; its opener is clearly not in an urgent state. Eira holds her breath and clings to one of her wrists with her other hand. The Archman stands by with his typical idle stillness, though he keeps a cursory hand hovering beside the rapier on his hip.

The door creaks open to reveal Glynis, a woman of a striking resemblance to Eira, their likeness most notable in the dark ebony hair, rounded jaw, and full lips which they both share. However, Glynis's features are noticeably more aged than Eira's: Glynis's hair is of a much duller shade of black, and the skin around her jaw and nose creases slightly. One feature which they clearly do not share are the dark rings beneath Glynis's eyes, the product of many sleepless nights accumulating over several weeks.

Glynis's tired eyes suddenly widen with a cataclysmic shock. She raises a hand to cover her mouth, a gesture which had been vicariously handed down to Eira. A cacophony of confusion, solace, and disbelief wracks her mercilessly. She is not sure whether she is beginning to hallucinate from the many hours of lost sleep. It seems far too miraculous to have her abducted daughter suddenly appear on her doorstep like this.

"Eira...?" Glynis speaks barely above a hush. Not able to rely upon her visual senses to accurately portray reality, Glynis steps forwards and reaches a quivering hand outwards, fully ready to have it pass through her daughter as though she were made of air and light.

Eira reaches out a consoling hand and takes her mother's palm in her own, holding her gently. An immense relief washes over Glynis as she steps forward and pulls Eira in towards her, hugging her daughter with unabashed closeness.

Eira can feel weeks of anxiety and dread melt off her mother, evaporating into the air around them. Glynis's embrace has a nearly crushing force behind it, but her frail stature prevents her from causing any real discomfort.

"I...I thought..." Glynis's voice can hardly keep itself together. Her breathing hitches as she starts to cry with overwhelming joy.

"It's good to see you, mother." Eira returns the embrace wholeheartedly, feeling tears welling up in her eyes as well.

Glynis wipes the drops of liquid worry from her eyes, only now taking notice of the Archman's presence. It seems impossible that she could have overlooked him so easily, given his large frame and height, but Eira's presence took priority over every other thing in existence.

Glynis pulls away from Eira slowly, but keeps a hand connected to her forearm. She turns to the Archman, who has yet to move from his spot or change expressions.

"I don't believe we've met..." Glynis wipes the last bits of moisture from her eyes as she speaks. "Were you the one who rescued my daughter?"

"Not exactly," the Archman says with a dry tone.

Glynis pauses, her confusion starting to return in modicum increments. She looks between Eira and the Archman and spots the collar around Eira's neck. The chain connected to it rests firmly in the Archman's grip.

"Are you..." Glynis holds Eira's arm tighter, slowly pulling her away from the Archman. She surveys his monolithic appearance, only now starting to notice his eclectic features: red eyes, silver hair, and an aura which saps the strength from those who observe him.

"You..." She pieces together who is standing before her and, more importantly, who is standing behind her daughter. Her shock returns almost full-force, along with a fresh sense of distress and uneasiness.

"That's *him*, isn't it?! What is he doing here?!" Glynis looks back and forth between Eira and the Archman with a confounded desperation.

"It's complicated..." Eira tries to explain, though she does not even know how to begin.

"Why...why has..." Glynis grapples with the circumstances she finds herself in, her bewilderment quickly turning into a defensive rage.

"I'm here to see your husband," the Archman responds calmly, not responding at all to Glynis's flustered state, which is growing more malicious by the second.

"I don't care what business you have with us! If you don't leave us be right now, I'll have your head put on a spike!" Glynis walks up to the Archman with a vicious indignation, paying little mind to the massive height disparity between the two of them.

"Somehow I doubt that." The Archman looks down at Glynis, replying with an indifferent stillness.

"Mother, please just—" Eira tries to interject, but she is quickly cut off, as Glynis continues her diatribe towards the uncaring Archman.

"If it's forgiveness you've come to ask for, then I have nothing to offer you! How dare you show your face—"

"I was the one who asked him here!" Eira inserts herself between Glynis and the Archman much more forcefully this time.

Glynis steps back with a baffled look about her. This situation has only grown more and more discombobulating with each passing second. "You did?"

"He can help cure Father! That's why he's here!" Eira places a hand on the Archman's arm with a protective gesture.

"What?" Glynis looks back at the Archman. She retains much of her scepticism, but seeing Eira defending the Archman's character inspires a perplexing reassurance.

"You can?" Glynis stares down the Archman, asking her question at a heavily interrogative angle.

"I can't make any promises," he responds logically.

"Is Father alright?" Eira looks to her mother with a tense concern.

"He doesn't have much time left..." Glynis says with solemn energy. She takes Eira's hand and guides her towards the door. "I'll bring you to him."

"Hold on." The Archman places a hand on Eira's shoulder, halting her in place. "She stays with me."

"Excuse me?" Glynis looks back at the Archman.

"She's a valuable piece of collateral. She stays with me," he says with an indomitable clarity.

Glynis glares at the Archman with a contemptuous fervour behind her eyes. She speaks with a reserved malevolence. "What did you just say?"

"Mother, it's okay, he won't hurt anyone." Eira tries to defuse the antagonism in the air as best she can.

"He's the Archman! All he does is cause harm!" Glynis assaults the Archman with her words mercilessly, as a physical assault would evidently be unwise.

"That's..." Eira starts speaking but is unsure how to continue. "It'll be fine, I promise."

Glynis fumes, trying to keep her anger directed towards the Archman as she speaks to Eira. "Why on earth should I trust him after everything he's done to you?!"

"Because...I do," Eira responds with a quiet directness.

"You..." Glynis stares at Eira, completely baffled.

"He saved my life. More than once, actually," Eira explains, trying to strike a balance between a mediating softness and an assertive firmness. "And he can help Father as well."

Glynis closes her eyes, trying to contend with Eira's logic. She submits to a certain degree but raises another point in response.

"He's beyond help, Eira. There's nothing left we can do."

"That's not true! The Archman is an expert on mortal diseases. If anyone can help, it's him."

The Archman looks down to Eira, his statuesque expression coming to life for a brief moment.

Glynis turns to the Archman, maintaining her defensive front, but giving way enough for him to speak. "Are you really able to help?"

"Again, I can't make any promises. Let me examine him, and I'll see what I can do," the Archman replies simply.

Glynis keeps her glare fixated on him as she relinquishes control of the situation, though she retains a sizeable amount of scepticism.

"Very well, then." Glynis turns around and opens the door. She goes to enter with Eira, but the Archman keeps her in place.

"May I come in?" he enquires politely.

Glynis shifts her sights back to the Archman, puzzled by his uncharacteristic decorum.

"He needs an invitation before entering someone's property," Eira explains, trying not to make it sound like she is speaking about the Archman as though he were absent.

"Fine. Come in," Glynis says with deliberate derision.

"Thank you," the Archman replies earnestly.

After Eira's heartfelt reunion and the Archman's disquieting introduction to the servant staff, they make their way through the homestead, up to the master bedroom.

Glynis opens the door to the large bedroom and enters first, keeping Eira close behind her. The Archman enters last, lowering his head to clear the doorframe.

The room is in the exact same state that Eira left it in. Her father, Idris, is lying in the exact same spot as when she last saw him, beneath a thick wool blanket in the king-size bed. The latter takes up the majority of the room's floor space.

Eira, Glynis, and the Archman all approach the side of the bed with a solemn quietude. Idris is fast asleep, one arm at his side, the other resting on his stomach. Though he is in the same location as when Eira last saw him, he is in a considerably worse condition. His greying hair is thinning around its roots, and his face is plastered with a gaunt lack of colour. The skin around his neck and collarbone is beginning to show more bone than muscle, evidently from a significant amount of weight loss. If not for the slight rising and falling of his chest, he could easily be mistaken for a corpse. He has maybe a few weeks left, if at all.

Eira feels her heart sink as she looks upon her father. He is a rapidly decaying relic of his former self. Even when he had first contracted this malady, there was an unbreakable optimism which he kept with steadfast consistency. Looking at him in his current state, however, it would be impossible to assume any kind of hopefulness. Eira shifts her gaze to the only place where hope could be found: the Archman.

Glynis leans over Idris and places a careful hand on his shoulder to rouse him as gently as possible. Idris gradually opens his eyes, an act which seems so simple in execution, and yet it demands an incredible amount of effort from him. It takes him several seconds to adjust to his surroundings, blinking with a concerted laboriousness. When his eyes have calibrated enough to the room's faint lighting, he looks up at Glynis, then turns his attention to one of the extra figures standing at his bedside. His eyelids suddenly separate from one another with immense disbelief.

"Eira—" Idris only manages to get two syllables out before he is interrupted by a vehement coughing from his lungs, causing him to contort his body and shudder with agitated discomfort. After a series of violent wheezes, Idris rests his head back down, with his wife's assistance.

"Don't strain yourself, dear," Glynis speaks softly.

Idris turns back towards Eira, moving just his eyes to look upon her. For just a single magical moment, there is alleviation from his debilitating sickness.

"Is...is that really you, Eira?" A trickle of blood runs out of the corner of Idris's mouth, but he pays it no mind.

"It's me, Father." Eira kneels down at her father's side and takes his hand in a familiar clutch. She wishes she could lean in and embrace him, but she knows it would put too much pressure on his frail body.

Though Idris's face is much too exhausted to convey anything other than illness, his eyes begin to water with monumental relief. His reaction inspires a similar response in Eira and Glynis, who vicariously experience the sudden abatement of suffering from someone whom they both love.

Idris's warm gaze freezes with an abrupt coldness as he catches a glimpse of the Archman, who looks down at Idris with an ambience of stony coldness. Idris begins to wonder if he did not wake up at all and is instead being greeted by death itself.

"Who...who are you?" Idris's raspy voice says with a petrified stiffness.

"He's here to help," Eira explains softly, speaking to Idris but trying to convince both her parents.

The Archman steps up next to Idris, removes the cloth bag from his back, and opens it. He rummages through it silently, much to Idris's tense discontentment. After a few seconds, the Archman procures an instrument from the bag: a small metal cup connected to a pair of rubberised tubes that end in a pair of stiff plugs. The Archman fits the device around his neck, then turns to Eira and Glynis.

"I'll need you to sit him up and remove his shirt."

Eira and Glynis follow the Archman's directives. They pull back the bedspread, help Idris to a sitting position with much caution, then slowly unbutton and remove his dark grey shirt.

The Archman fits the two plugs of the device into his ears, then takes the metal cup and places it on Idris's back. He shifts the cup around slightly, making a silent analysis as Eira and Glynis keep Idris sitting upright.

"Breath in," the Archman instructs.

Idris inhales slowly, trying his best not to cough. He fills his lungs most of the way, but as he goes to exhale the biting ache quickly returns to his pulmonary organs, causing him to hack several times. After the ordeal has concluded, there is a light spattering of blood on the bedsheets.

The Archman continues to move the metal cup around Idris's back, not appearing to react at all to the devastating coughs. He listens intently until he is satisfied, then removes the plugs from his ears and hangs the medical instrument back around his neck.

"You can let him down now."

Eira and Glynis lower him back down to a resting position, moving him as delicately as they can. The Archman looks over Idris, continuing his analysis in his head.

"Weakness, fever, pain in the chest, lack of appetite, night sweats. Are those symptoms accurate?" he asks.

"That's...yes..." Idris replies with as little effort as necessary.

“Well, that went much faster than expected.” The Archman stands up and turns to Glynis. “You suspect it is the white plague, correct?”

“That’s what many doctors have suggested, yes.” Glynis says with a curt nod.

“That appears to be the case here. Tuberculosis.” The Archman raises a hand to his chin as he vocalises his conclusion.

“What’s that?” Eira probes, both eager and hesitant to understand the illness better.

“An infection of the lungs. Pests so small they can’t be seen by the naked eye,” the Archman elucidates. “The fact he’s still alive is nothing short of a miracle.”

“How much longer does he have?” Glynis asks reluctantly.

The Archman returns his medical apparatus to the cloth bag, closes it definitively, and makes his way to the door.

“After I’m done with him, as long as it will take for old age to claim him.”

CHAPTER Eighteen

A NOCTURNAL DISCOURSE

A few sparse rays of moonlight pierce through the cracks between a pair of curtains, cutting into the dark bedroom. Any light provided by the moonlight is rendered inconsequential, however, as a lit candle on the bedside table overpowers the natural luminescence of the moon.

Eira lies in her bed, eyes closed, her back facing towards the candle. It has been over a month since she has slept in her own bed and she had been expecting to reacclimate to the setting almost immediately, but strangely enough that is not the case. There is no doubt that the room she had slept in her entire life provides a certain kind of nostalgic comfort, but it is not the same as the bed on the Archman's ship. For one thing, the complete darkness of the Archman's bedroom made it quite easy to fall asleep, a luxury which she did not realise she was taking for granted. Even the feel of her bed is different, though. What it possesses in familiarity, it lacks in novelty. It has a much more worn-in texture to it which easily sinks under her weight. The Archman's bed is much more rigid and sturdy, evidently built to support someone of the Archman's stature. It is also noticeably larger.

There are at least still a few reminiscent elements that make the sudden transition more bearable. The cold grip of the steel collar around Eira's neck is something she has gotten so used to sleeping with that it would probably be challenging to go without it. Additionally, the Archman's silent but noticeable presence in the space eases her nerves considerably.

He is sitting next to the bedside table with a booklet in one hand and a quill in the other, scrawling upon the pages of the booklet with intermittent strokes. The candlelight reflects off the Archman's glasses, which rest on the bridge of his nose.

Though Eira has her back turned to him, it is as if she can see him with perfect clarity, the orange glow of the candle casting a warm light on his scintillating hair. Eira feels an urge to turn around and refresh the image in her mind, but she stays put. She has been lying still for several minutes now to give the impression of being asleep, and she does not want to break the illusion. She is not sure exactly what she has to gain from this little thespian trickery, but she continues to do so regardless.

The Archman sets down his booklet and quill, then stands up from the chair. He turns around and blows out the candle, making the dim moonlight the only source of light in the room.

Eira focuses all her attention on her sense of hearing, as it is now the only way of determining movement within the space. She can hear him walk a few paces, then come to a halt. There are a few seconds of nothing, until Eira feels a corner of the bed sink down considerably. Eira deduces that he must have taken a seat on the bed, though she has yet to discern a reason for this action.

Through the pitch blackness of the room, Eira can feel the Archman's gaze upon her. It has such a unique quality to it that she is beginning to recognise it without needing to even see it.

After a few seconds of silence, she feels a light touch on her shoulder. She had been anticipating some kind of contact from him, and yet it still took her off guard when he placed his hand upon her. His touch is muted slightly from the many layers of fabric between his palm and her shoulder, but she can still feel the intention behind it. There is a kind of soft delicacy to the gesture, which does not convey anything more than an acknowledgement of the connection between the two of them. It seems contradictory that a hand which is so adept at mutilation and vivisection can be so comforting, and yet that is precisely the effect it has.

The Archman removes his hand and stands up from the bed, though his touch lingers for several moments on Eira's shoulder. He makes his way towards the door and exits promptly. When she hears the door close shut, Eira opens her eyes.

One floor down, there is a subtle bustling as a pair of bodies move about in the permeating darkness. They congregate next to a window in a dining room, so they can see one another through the faint moonlight. It is Glynis and a young female servant, the sprightliest of the entire servant staff.

Glynis hands a closed envelope to the young servant, who receives it carefully.

"Where to, ma'am?" the young servant asks as quietly as is audibly possible.

"Straight to Commodore Kinsley. I don't have time for the postal service. Make sure you hand it to him directly," Glynis orders, her assertiveness coming across clearly despite speaking at a whisper.

The servant nods and leaves quickly, her footfalls disappearing into the darkness.

Glynis stands with her hands crossed over her stomach, breathing a light sigh of relief as she looks through the window and sees the servant leaving the premises.

Glynis quickly inhales the stress back into her body as she hears a new pair of footfalls coming down the staircase to the main floor. The unique metal-on-wood sound immediately indicates to her who it is. She closes the curtains to the window and straightens her posture, looking for something to make herself appear busy. She opts to take a seat at the dining table, assuming enough of a sombre attitude to give her a brooding quality.

The footfalls come closer, stopping just outside the dining room. A pair of crimson orbs float in the darkness, standing in the doorway of the room. Glynis looks up to the pair of blood-red irises, trying not to let them disturb her as much as they do.

"Is she asleep?" Glynis attempts to ignore the nightmarish qualities of the Archman's appearance by speaking to him as though he were just an ordinary guest.

"Yes." The Archman steps into the dinning room, half of his face illuminating slightly from the sparse moonlight.

Meanwhile, Eira tiptoes out of her bedroom, holding the chain delicately so that it does not rattle behind her. She steps out of the bedroom and makes her way to the top of the staircase, where she reaches the end of her chain. Though she is not able to travel any further, she can still make out Glynis and the Archman's words from the dining room at the bottom of the staircase. Eira is not fond of all the lurking and eavesdropping she has started doing recently, but her curiosity compels her with much more force than her reservations.

"I'll be taking her with me to the ship tomorrow." The Archman sits down at the dining table, in the chair diagonal from Glynis.

"What?!" Glynis's voice raises with a sharp crescendo.

"I told you, she stays with me. All my resources and materials are on my ship."

Glynis balls a hand into a fist beneath the table. She is finding it increasingly challenging to regard the Archman as a mere guest.

"You're welcome to come with her if you like," the Archman suggests.

Glynis pauses, taken aback by the genuine earnestness coming from the Archman. She quickly dismisses it, however, so she can rebuke him less hesitantly.

"So you can take another hostage, is that it?"

"Please, I can hardly contend with your daughter. Two of you would be far too much to handle," the Archman says with a dismissive ease. He leans on one of his hands, taking a contemplative position. "On second thought, perhaps I don't want you coming aboard..."

"I'm not going anywhere near your bloody ship, and neither is she," Glynis states adamantly.

"Suit yourself, but Eira stays with me," the Archman rebuts sternly. "That's my condition for your husband's recovery."

Glynis's knuckles start turning white beneath the table. She wants desperately to reject the Archman, but knows it is beyond futile. She releases the anger from her hands, bringing one of them up to her head to lean her face into.

"Why can't you just let my daughter be?" Glynis's voice is dense with an agonised tension.

Eira crouches down at the top of the staircase, listening as intensely as she can to the conversation.

"I told you why. She's a necessary piece of collateral—"

"Haven't you tormented her enough yet?" Glynis removes her hands from her face. Her corneas are glistening with a foreboding moisture, but it does not manage to escape her eyes. The last thing she wants is to cry in front of such a tremendous foe.

"I..." The Archman hesitates. "It's not my intention."

"Regardless, it's the effect you have on her."

"She's tormented by me?" The cold resilience of the Archman's voice fractures for a split second.

"Of course she is!" Glynis fumes, some of the tears slipping from her eyes as she leans in towards the Archman. "Abducting her in the night, keeping her in irons...don't you realise how cruel that is?!"

The Archman sits in silence, taking in Glynis's scathing utterances.

"No...I shouldn't expect you to understand," she continues, wiping the water from her eyes.

"I understand," the Archman retorts.

"Do you?! Then why take her in the first place?!"

The Archman turns his scarlet gaze downwards, looking at the table.

"I'm sorry..." he mutters under his breath. "I didn't mean to concern you so much."

"I'm not the one you should be apologising to."

The Archman nods his head, keeping his gaze down.

"I won't be bothering her much longer. I promise."

Glynis looks at the Archman in his semi-prostrated pose. It is an odd sight to behold, one which takes her off guard. She turns away, ending the conversation before she feels sympathy for him.

"Good."

Eira hears the Archman stand up from his seat, prompting her to quickly but silently return to her room, gathering the length of chain with her as she goes. She makes it back to her bed and pulls the covers up to her shoulders. There did not seem to be any crucial exchange of information between her mother and the Archman, but his concluding remark has a lingering effect on Eira which does not leave her mind until she falls asleep.

"Just a minute!" Eira hollers through her bedroom door as she digs frenetically through her wardrobe. Despite having gotten up relatively early, she was expecting to have more time to prepare herself before leaving with the Archman. Evidently there is no such thing as early or late for someone who spends entire years awake.

"You said that over a minute ago," the Archman replies from the other side of the door.

Glynis stands by idly as the Archman knocks on the door, holding his cloth bag. If it were not for his compulsive need for a verbal invitation, he certainly would have barged in several minutes ago.

Eira opens the door and briskly steps out. The Archman opens his mouth to admonish her for her tardiness one final time, but he halts before speaking a word. Eira is wearing practical but elegant attire: a long-sleeved dress made with light fabrics, ideal for summer weather, and a pair of tight, brown leather boots with a small heel built in. It is nowhere near as expensive as the dress her parents had bought her months prior, though it is significantly more impressive than the assorted outfits she has had to cobble together from the Archman's massive collection.

The Archman looks down at her and closes his mouth, taking a full second to observe her. He had not really taken a proper look at her in clothing that actually fit her. Glynis notices him looking for half a second, before snapping himself to attention.

"Great, let's go." The Archman takes the chain attached to Eira's collar and gathers it up with one hand; his other hand is holding his cloth bag. He turns to Glynis, his hands continuing to move as he speaks.

"The offer still stands. You're welcome to join us."

Glynis ponders temperamentally before giving her response.

"I suppose there's no chance you'll reconsider."

"Correct."

Eira, Glynis, and the Archman make their way out of the household, exit through the front door, and walk down a stone path, which quickly turns into the dirt road leading out of the property.

They walk together in silence; Glynis and the Archman are on either side of Eira. After about an hour of strolling, Glynis's pace starts to become more of a light amble, then eventually a lagging trudge. She soon comes to a stop and leans over, breathing heavily. She evidently has not walked this much in quite some time.

Eira and the Archman look back at her. She has yet to catch her breath.

"Mother? Are you okay?" Eira places a tender hand on Glynis's back.

"I...just need a moment," Glynis says though deep inhales and exhales.

"I'd rather not." The Archman walks over to Glynis, stoops down in front of her, then grabs her with one hand and lifts her up over his shoulder in one swift motion, catching both Glynis and Eira off guard.

"AH!!! PUT ME DOWN!!!" Glynis grabs the Archman's back with a panicked grip.

"No thanks."

"UNHAND ME!!!"

The Archman ignores her and resumes their trek, carrying his cloth bag and bundle of chain in one hand and steadying Glynis over his shoulder with the other hand. The additional weight does not seem to slow him down in the slightest.

Glynis tries to continue her resistance, but she is completely devoid of energy. The Archman's stabilising hand on her lower back provides enough reassurance that she will not fall, but what she objects to is the humiliation of being carried in such a manner. With her frail constitution, however, it quickly becomes clear that she cannot stage any proper rebuke against the Archman. She decides to stop retaliating but makes it clear throughout the walk that she is still quite upset.

When they arrive at the docks, the Archman sets Glynis back down on her feet, giving her a moment to find her balance.

"Here we are." The Archman walks towards the gangplank leading up to the deck of his ship.

Glynis looks up at the Archman's ship, her eyes immediately widening with awe.

CHAPTER Nineteen

AN ADVERSE LIBERATION

"I'd offer a tour, but we've got a bit of a time constraint." The Archman walks through the lower decks of the ship, Eira and Glynis in tow. Glynis looks at the lanterns installed across the ship, fascinated by the unflinching consistency with which they illuminate the space. Eira looks to her mother, wondering if she had the same expression when she first stepped onto the Archman's vessel.

They stop before a closed door at the Archman's behest, as he pulls the key ring from a belt compartment. Eira recognises this door as the only one that was locked shut, except for the cells inside the brig.

"Just a quick detour." The Archman opens the door and steps inside, illuminating one of the lamps.

Eira and Glynis take a single pace into the room, not daring to venture another step further. The walls of the room are lined with a massive assortment of weapons: a variety of swords and cutting implements, and dozens of firearms, ranging from small handheld pistols to large long-distance rifles. There is no need to ask why this room is kept under lock and key.

The Archman walks over to a dresser and pulls it open. The inside is filled with silver canisters, which Eira immediately recognises as the kind that releases that crippling white gas that the Archman had used aboard Kinsley's ship. The corner of the drawer is the only spot not occupied by silver canisters; a leather mask resides there instead. It has a pair of smoked glass circles covering the eye holes and a thick steel filter over the mouth. The mask presents quite a horrifying visage, much more so when it is appearing in the wake of a cloud of deadly white gas.

Eira thinks back to that night she first met the Archman. It is hard to believe that he is the same person who had been behind that terrifying mask.

The Archman takes the mask under his arm and extinguishes the lanterns before leaving with Eira and Glynis. He locks the door, then guides them through the corridors until they arrive at the study. He pushes the door open and walks inside, locking the chain around the foot of the desk.

Glynis and Eira step into the room together. Glynis continues to be absolutely astonished by everything she comes across. She tries to keep her reactions more reserved at first but quickly gives up on it. There are simply too many beguiling sights. She feels like she has stepped into a different century.

The study is familiar enough compared to the many other technologically astounding features of the ship, though it is still impressive in its sheer magnitude.

The Archman goes to the door and turns back to Eira and Glynis before exiting. "Keep yourselves entertained here for the day. I'll come get you when I'm done."

Glynis looks about the study, trying to find a single vertical surface that is not occupied with bookshelves. "Where did he acquire all these?"

"He didn't. They're all his own works." Eira walks over to the closest bookshelf and starts sifting through the many works.

"All of them?" Glynis tries not to sound as amazed as she actually is.

"He's been alive for thousands of years."

"That would explain it..."

The Archman steps into a dark chamber, sets down his cloth bag and leather mask, and turns on a few lanterns to push away the darkness. The room is dustier than the rest of the ship, having been neglected for the past few months. There are dozens of glass beakers and containers strewn about the space, which the Archman starts sorting through, collecting the few ones necessary for the procedure. He brings them to an isolated countertop in the centre of the room, then starts opening cabinets and drawers, pulling out a variety of substances kept in glass tubes and bottles. After several minutes, there is a miscellaneous gathering of translucent liquids and white powders laid out across the countertop. The Archman double-checks his materials, then pulls his booklet out of the cloth bag, and flips it open to the appropriate page. He puts his leather gas mask on and secures it to his head, readying himself to begin.

"COMMODORE KINSLEY HAS BEEN WORRIED SICK ABOUT you."

Eira looks up from the book in her hands, shifting her gaze over to her mother. She is not sure how to react to the unprompted comment.

"So I've heard."

"He feels awful that you were taken while under his care. He told me he wouldn't rest until you'd been rescued."

Eira feels a dreadful question surface in her consciousness.

"Mother...what will happen to the Archman if they catch him?"

"I can't say for certain...but I'm sure they will impart all possible means of cruelty."

Eira looks down at the book in her hands, using it as a distraction from the aching sensation in her chest.

Glynis walks over to Eira and places a hand on her shoulder.

"It will all be over soon, dear."

MANY HOURS LATER, THE ARCHMAN RETURNS TO THE study. No words are exchanged as he unlocks Eira from the desk and guides her and Glynis out from below decks. They step out onto the main deck as the sun begins to set on the horizon, casting a deep orange on the landscape. The Archman looks out across the water and pulls back the hood of his cloak. This twilight hour is one of the few times of day he can tolerate the sunlight. He walks with Eira and Glynis across the deck, arriving at the gangplank leading down to the dock. He stops and rummages through his cloth bag and pulls out a small glass jar. An off-white powder fills most of it.

"Here." He hands it to Glynis.

"Is…is this it?" She holds the glass container with a delicate curiosity.

"That's it. There's enough for four months there. Give him two teaspoons a week until it runs out. Keep administering it even if he starts to recover, otherwise he could relapse," the Archman instructs as directly as he can.

"Thank you." Eira feels an impulse to embrace the Archman, but decides against it, given her mother's presence.

The Archman turns to Eira. His face has its usual icy stillness to it, but the empty indifference which always rests behind his eyes is nowhere to be found.

"Consider this my apology," the Archman says softly.

"We'll receive your apology so long as this concoction works," Glynis says with a harsh scepticism.

"Follow my instructions, and it will. You have my word," the Archman retorts.

A faint silence sets in among the three of them as they arrive at a crossroads.

"Before we go, can I say goodbye to my father?" Eira turns to the Archman.

"That won't be necessary." The Archman goes to a compartment on his belt and pulls out the key ring.

"What?" Eira mutters.

The Archman takes one of the keys on the ring and walks over to her. He takes hold of the collar around her neck and inserts the key into the lock. With a quick twist, the metal shackle opens. Eira and Glynis are both taken aback as the Archman removes the restraining device from Eira.

"You're free to go."

Eira freezes solid, her mouth hanging ever so slightly ajar. She is not sure what she is feeling. It is much too complex to comprehend.

"I am?" Her voice quivers with a deep unsteadiness. "But... what about Kinsley?"

"I have the Raeburn's protection," the Archman explains as logically as he can. "I can't keep you captive any longer. It's not safe for you here."

"What dangers could possibly threaten us?" Eira asks with an agitated confusion.

"External threats don't concern me." The Archman grits his teeth, trying to keep himself composed. "But...I'm worried that I might harm you myself."

"Oh..." Eira lowers her head.

"Eira, let's go." Glynis takes her by the arms, coaxing her towards the gangplank. For a second she feels an impulse to thank the Archman, but she quickly stifles it. She wants to leave this place as soon as possible.

Eira pauses, then takes her mother's hand off her arm.

"You go ahead. I want to say goodbye."

Glynis is taken aback by Eira's request, but she humours it with a mistrustful reservation. She walks down the length of the gangplank to the dock.

Eira waits until her mother is out of earshot, then turns back to the Archman. She looks up at him, seeing a few beads of moisture forming in the corners of his crimson eyes. It inspires a similar reaction in her own eyes.

"Thank you for helping my father." She averts her gaze, finding it increasingly challenging to speak clearly.

"It was the least I could do," the Archman says with a cold humbleness.

Eira works up the courage to look back towards him. She takes a final look at his mythical features: his blood-red eyes, scintillating silver hair, and the few sparse scars laden across his white skin. The aching sensation in her stomach that first appeared when she was granted her freedom starts to aggravate itself as she looks at him for the last time.

"Goodbye...Archman." She speaks just above a whisper.

The Archman cracks a light smile, blinking a few times to keep the tears in his eyes from accumulating. He takes a breath in, expending a significant amount of energy in order to speak.

"My name is Adrulac."

Eira does not react for a full second, until she smiles as well, letting out a light chortle. "How on earth was I meant to guess that?"

"You weren't." Adrulac laughs along with Eira.

The lighthearted atmosphere quickly dies down back to its sombre default.

"I guess we won't be able to finish our wager." Eira comments off-handedly.

"I guess not."

Eira and Adrulac take a final moment to look at each other. She looks back at her mother, who is staring up at them with unwavering intent. Her impulse from earlier returns, but this time she gives into it fully, stepping forwards and wrapping her arms around Adrulac. She leans her head into his chest, until she is close enough to feel his heartbeat. All the folklore asserts that he does not have one, but clearly this is erroneous.

He encircles Eira and holds her tightly to him. They are both grateful for the positioning of their bodies, as it allows them to hide their faces from one another. They both close their eyes and try to fight back the tears. Their sporadic breathing is easily felt by one another, though, making it evident that neither of them are in a tranquil state.

Adrulac leans his head down and plants a single kiss on Eira's forehead.

"Goodbye, princess."

Eira squeezes him for a few more moments, trying to extract the last bit of joy from their embrace. His touch eases the ache in her stomach slightly, but the fact that it will come to an inevitable end keeps it from being purged completely.

Adrulac pulls away from Eira and looks down at her with a sombre gaze.

"Tell your mother to find a better husband for you."

Eira nods a few times. She knows that if she tries to speak, she will undoubtedly start crying.

Adrulac steps back, releasing her from his grip after a month of having had her in his grasp. Eira turns and walks down the gangplank swiftly. She knows the longer she lingers, the harder it will be to let go.

She arrives next to her mother on the dock, as Adrulac hoists the gangplank back up to the deck of his ship. He looks down over the edge of the deck, catching a final glimpse of Eira before disappearing from her sights.

"Come, Eira." Glynis places a hand on her shoulder, turning to leave the dock.

"Not yet." Eira stays put, her feet rooted like tree trunks. Glynis has not seen this level of resistance from her before. She removes her hand from her daughter and stands by silently. Eira looks out from the dock as Adrulac's ship lowers its sails and pulls away, slowly getting further and further away.

With each bit of distance that grows between Eira and Adrulac, the ache in her stomach grows more and more severe. Her whole body is tremoring as she tries to process the deluge of sadness and confusion plaguing her.

"Eira?" Glynis steps forwards, trying to get her daughter's attention.

In that moment, Eira knows that she will never be able to properly process the torment she finds herself in. There is only one thing which can alleviate it, and it is currently sailing away from her.

"Mother..." Eira turns to Glynis, tears streaming down both her eyes. "...I'm sorry."

Before Glynis can respond in any way, Eira leaps off the edge of the dock, plunging into the water beneath.

"EIRA?!" Glynis gasps in shock.

Eira resurfaces and starts swimming towards the departing ship. She is weighed down heavily by the fabric of her dress, but she presses onwards. She exerts herself more than she ever has with anything else in her life.

Adrulac hears Glynis's surprised holler coming from the dock and walks over to the edge of the upper deck. He looks over it curiously, immediately taken aback as he sees Eira swimming towards him. He quickly gets over his initial shock, shaking his head to return himself to the present moment. He rushes over to the steering wheel and pulls a lever, dropping the ship's anchor. He makes a mad dash over the railing of the upper deck and lands on the main deck with a loud impact. The stairs would have been much too slow. He quickly removes his large cloak and metal-toed boots as he runs up to the edge of the ship. He grabs a rope secured to the banister of the ship and tosses it overboard, before leaping over himself. He dives dexterously into the chilly evening water and quickly makes his way towards Eira.

Eira's initial surge of energy is starting to wane. She is beginning to feel the weight of her soaked clothing more and more with each stroke, her head starting to submerge intermittently. She is not even sure if she is going in the right direction. The rising panic in her body quickly disperses as she feels Adrulac's arms wrap themselves under her shoulders. He starts pulling her towards the ship, keeping her head above the surface of the water until they reach the rope dangling from the banister.

Eira grabs onto the rope with one hand, her other clinging to Adrulac's shoulder. He does the same, gripping the rope with his hand and encircling his other arm around her waist to keep her from slipping beneath the surface.

"What...what are you doing?" Adrulac tilts his head to the side quickly, flicking his damp silver hair out of his eyes so he can see Eira better.

"I don't know..." She tries to think as she catches her breath.

There is a look of relief and ease about him, though it is bogged down by a persistent hesitancy. "I thought I told you... so long as you're with me, I can't guarantee your safety."

Eira looks at Adrulac, noticing his damp locks slowly falling back over his face. She lifts her hand from his shoulder and pushes the few strands of silver aside with her middle and index finger, fully revealing his sparsely scarred face to her. She cannot help but smile.

"I don't happen to share your concerns."

Eira's hazel eyes reflect off Adrulac's crimson ones, the droplets of water from their faces creating an enticing atmosphere. Though the location is far from optimal, they know that they cannot wait. They both lean in towards one another, kissing each other with a deep passion, alleviating the aggravation brought on by their separation. Beneath the water, they slowly start to wrap their legs around one another to hold themselves together, as their hands are busy clinging to the rope to keep them afloat.

They know that if they let go from one another, they will surely sink back into the cold depths.

TO BE CONTINUED IN BOOK 3: SAVAGE SALVATION

www.ingramcontent.com/pod-product-compliance
Lightning Source LLC
LaVergne TN
LVHW020717110826
845149LV00012B/2305

* 9 7 8 1 0 6 9 2 0 9 3 2 0 *